CHANGE YOUR MIND
AND
CHANGE YOUR LIFE

CHANGE YOUR MIND AND CHANGE YOUR LIFE

A Step-by-Step
Guide to Letting Go
of Your Past

Zoilita Grant

Founder of Hypnotic Coaching-Certified by the International
Association of Counselors and Therapists

CITIOFBOOKS, INC.
3736 Eubank NE Suite A1
Albuquerque, NM 87111-3579
www.citiofbooks.com
Hotline 1 (877) 389-2759
Fax: 1 (505) 930-7244

Ordering Information:
Quantity sales. Special discounts are available on quantity purchases by corporations, associations, and others. For details, contact the publisher at the address above.

Printed in the United States of America.

ISBN-13:   Softcover   979-8-89391-197-8
             eBook   979-8-89391-198-5

Library of Congress Control Number: 2024914336

CONTENTS

DEDICATION

This book is dedicated to you who seek to improve the quality of your life. May your quest for self-improvement be filled with reliance, curiosity, and your unwavering commitment to your personal growth. I celebrate you who dare to dream, strive for positive change, and believe in your own limitless potential. Your journey matters and may these words serve as a guiding light on your journey. You have a right to redefine your past, to rewrite your stories and break free from the chains of the past. When you are willing to explore self-discovery, you can move from reacting to making choices. You are free to create a life that is rich and fulfilling. By learning to utilize the power of your mind you will learn to create your life by design.

Blessings, Zoilita

ACKNOWLEDGEMENTS

Ariela Wilcox, The Wilcox Agency-Literary Agent and the #1 U.S. Expert in Leveraging through Licensing. The Wilcox Agency 1155 Camino Del Mar Suite 173 Del Mar, California 92014

Laura Schwamman, is an independent designer, illustrator, and art director outside of Denver, Colorado. She focuses on graphic design, custom lettering and illustration.

lauraschwamman@gmail.com
E-MAIL: laura.schwamman@gmail..com
https://www@lauraschwammandesign.com/

Book Designer: MCD Advertising & Design 1590-D Rosecrans Ave # 201 Manhattan Beach, California 90266 PH: (310) 545-2233
E-Mail: david@mcd-adv@com

David Quigley Alchemy Institute
P.O. Box 206 4241 Montgomery Drive Santa Rosa, CA. 95405 PH: 707-888-8403
E-Mail: info@alchemyinsitute@com
https://www@alchemyinstitute.com/

ADVANCED PRAISE FOR CHANGE YOUR MIND AND CHANGE YOUR LIFE

I LOVE this book! **"Change Your Mind and Change Your Life"** is an insightful and thought-provoking journey in creating the life you're dreaming of. Zoilita has masterfully guided her readers to create the life they want by design, not by default. The steps she has created are practical and easy to follow. Zoilita not only gives us permission but provides motivation to change. This is a solutions-based approach that is informative and fun. Zoilita shares her expertise and wisdom, as well as compelling research to help us understand the "why" of our behaviors and habits. I love the gentle, supportive urging this book provides. After reading this book, you'll recognize how you're being your own worst enemy and how to become your own best friend, living the life of your dreams. If you're looking to make positive change, this is the book for you!

Nancy C.Ht, MHC- Hypnotic Coach

Change Your Mind and Change Your Life. A Step-by-Step Guide to Letting go of your Past is a jewel of tools that assist in changing into a happier life and more successful. The step-by-step guide is easy to fallow and to the point. Allowing the seeker to use the (mp3's) and get a better vision of their past and the blocks to success. Also, the tools and understanding that it is Possible to live a more fulfilling lifechanging the mind and changing the life. It totally has worked for me. A graduate for the class of 2002. My Business in Rochester, MN grew to other towns and nationally. Letting go of the Past blocks to living a Successful life is proof that this Works. Zoilita is a Master Teacher and Way shower, I cherish her guidance, teaching and friendship.

Rev. Mae Clayton CCHt, RMT-P, specializing in PTSD

Zoilita Grant's book **Change Your Mind and Change Your Life** has helped me navigate several personal and professional challenges. It is brimming with practical exercises to improve one's mindset and enable them to operate on a higher playing field. I think everyone should read it in order to achieve their ultimate life's goals. I couldn't recommend it more highly." Robert Licensed Acupuncturist

I've known and worked with Zoilita for a long time. She's an amazing coach, very insightful and effective; I've learned a great deal from her. Using the techniques she outlines in this wonderful book, I am more aware and intentional about the way I think, and my subconscious is activated, alive and well. Thank You Zoilita.!!!

Joseph MA LPC-Psychotherapist

"Weight Mastery lives in the accountability to ourselves." Zoilita's statement to me during a Coaching session was profound. After taking control of the "Committee", I had to tell the Rebel Child to stop self-sabotaging and become the adult I would be proud to be. Childhood can be treacherous, and we drag our hurt, shame and guilt into adulthood. However, the truth is that with a kind and loving Coach, meditation and challenging physical exercise, weight mastery is an attainable goal. "**Change Your Mind and Change Your Life**" is a great coaching instructional manual and workbook combination. This material helped quelled my years of anger, mind chatter, passive/ aggressive behaviors. While I continue to be a "work in progress" I have let go of the baggage from the past and continue to grow into a kinder happier 73-year-old adult. This material has re-shaped my life and those around me are a reflection of that growth.

Jean B.A. Retired Administrator

INTRODUCTION

How I Learned the Power of a Success Mindset

There is great power in the mind, and clearing subconscious blocks shifts the mindset and achieves goals. I stood on the scale today and weighed 125 lbs. A far cry from the 265 lbs. I weighed at 16. I climbed a 15,800 ft Mountain last year on my way to Machu Picchu.

When I was 16, I could barely walk up two flights of stairs. I used the power of my mind by learning hypnosis then and hypnotized myself to let go of 150 lbs. in a year. That is the moment that my journey as a coach began. I learned the power of mindset and how it can transform your life. I graduated from Berkely with a degree in Clinical Psychology and later got a master's in social work. After working in a couple of nonprofits, I became a psychotherapist.

Over the years I continued to be fascinated by meditation, hypnosis, and other mindful states. I did numerous training and certifications and integrated it into my psychotherapy practice. I loved psychotherapy but over the course of time outgrew the model. I wanted to work in a more empowering way with people. In 2008 I discovered coaching and realized that it was my real life calling. I did the basic International Coach Federation training and then pioneered and got accredited to a new branch of hypnosis called hypnotic coaching. Hypnotic coaching goes beyond problem solving and co-creates a life for you that is purposeful and focused. I will help you bridge the gap between where you are and where you want to be in your profession and personal life! I wrote this book to help people like you to experience the same degree of positive change that I and thousands that I have taught and worked with have. Change Your Mind and Change Your Life! Create by Design not Default. It worked for me. It will work for you!

Zoilita Grant

CHAPTER 1

CONQUERING STRESS

Life can be tough sometimes and stress always makes things worse. We can't avoid stress or ignore it but we can conquer it. Conquering stress means stress still exists, but it no longer controls you. Working with your mind is the most powerful tool for taking the power from stress and eliminating the symptoms of anxiety, depression, weight, and the addictions. Conquering stress will provide you the foundation to solve issues you have worked on for years. To begin this journey, the first step is to let of your past…your baggage. Experiences from our past can make life more stressful in different ways. If something bad or scary happened to us before, it might come back to bother us and make us feel stressed, even in different situations. Our past also affects how we automatically react to things around us. For example, if we had a hard time in the past, we might start feeling stressed when similar things happen again.

The way we think about our past experiences is also important. If we often think about bad things that happened, it can make us stressed. Our relationships with family and friends can also be a source of stress if we had problems with them before.

Often, if we didn't solve problems from the past, they can still make us feel stressed. The way we expect things to happen or the pressure we feel to be successful can also be linked to our past experiences. If we faced high expectations before, we might continue to feel stressed trying to meet those expectations.

Thinking too much about past mistakes or bad memories can add to stress. Also, stress can change the structure of our brain over time, making it more likely for us to feel stressed in the future. That is why I have provided all the stress management tools in this book. You can conquer stress, so it rolls off you like water off a duck's back.

Even though past experiences can make us stressed, it's important to know that you can learn ways to let go of your past. Talking to someone, practicing mindfulness, and finding positive ways to handle stress can help us handle life better.

The second step is recognizing that certain traits of your personality make stress have a greater effect on you. We are always our own worst enemy. This paves the way for anxiety, depression, panic, and phobias as well the coping symptoms of weight, smoking and the addictions. One of my goals is to help you become your best friend. It's important to learn the traits of a high anxiety personality and see which of these characteristics are true for you.

It is Important to know that meditation and self-hypnosis can assist in alleviating the symptoms, but true lasting relief demands a shift in how you perceive and respond to the world. Frequently, our reactions to life events can be disproportionate and provoke anxiety, insomnia, panic, or phobias. The line between feeling stressed and experiencing a full-blown panic attack is a matter of intensity and degree rather than a fundamental difference. Working with the mind can be beneficial for you regardless of the severity of your symptoms and condition.

The first step in learning to get rid of your symptoms is to learn how to create a safe place mental haven…. a safe space in your mind whenever you need a moment of calm, you can consciously relax and retreat to this safe place. The second step to work with the breath to reduce your stress level. The third step is to learn self-hypnosis and practicing it daily for relaxation which is essential. It's worth noting that one of the positive side effects of all meditation and hypnosis is stress reduction.

Types of Stress

Stress management can seem perplexing because there are various forms of stress: acute stress, episodic acute stress, and chronic stress. Each type has distinct characteristics, symptoms, durations, and approaches to treatment. Let's explore each type.

A. **Acute Stress**: This is most common form of stress, stemming from recent demands and anticipated future pressures. It can be thrilling and exciting in small doses but becomes exhausting when excessive. For example, skiing down a challenging slope is exhilarating initially but becomes tiring later in the day. Similarly, too much short-term stress can lead to psychological distress, tension headaches, upset stomach, and other common symptoms. Acute stress symptoms are typically recognizable, manifesting as emotional distress, muscular problems, stomach and bowel issues, and transient overarousal. The good news is that acute stress is treatable and manageable.

B. **Episodic Acute Stress:** Some individuals experience acute stress frequently, leading to a chaotic and crisis-ridden life. They rush but are often late, and everything seems to go wrong for them. These individuals are prone to irritability, anxiety, and tension, and their interpersonal relationships may deteriorate. Episodic acute stress can lead to conditions similar to those observed in Type A personalities, such as heart issues. Another form of episodic acute stress comes from ceaseless worrying, leading to symptoms like tension headaches and chest pain. Treating episodic acute stress often requires professional intervention and can be a lengthy process since it involves lifestyle changes.

C. **Chronic Stress:** This type of stress goes on year after year. It results from constant demands, feeling trapped in difficult situations, or early traumatic experiences. Chronic stress breaks down the immune system and can lead to health problems, including suicide, violence, heart disease, and more. The challenge with chronic stress is that people may become so accustomed to it that they ignore its presence. Ending chronic stress is complicated and involves both increasing yourself awareness and changing your lifestyle.

Stress is a personal experience, and what one person finds stressful, another may not. Stress can present both as emotional and physical tension, with physical stress often leading to emotional discomfort. Stress is pervasive in modern life, contributing to various serious health issues, including obesity, anxiety, insomnia, and depression. You encounter stress in different areas of your lives, including at work, on the road, and at home. However, you have the power to influence your stress response, either by changing your circumstances or by changing how you perceive and manage stress. It's natural for everyone to experience worry and fear at times, but if these emotions become overwhelming and interfere with daily life, meditation and hypnosis are valuable resources. High-anxiety personality traits can make you more susceptible to stress and all its effects. Be honest with yourself and vow to change. Make a plan and follow through.

Characteristics of a High Anxiety Personality

1. Rigid Thinking:

Rigid thinking is the tendency to perceive life as a series of either/or alternatives. Events are either right or wrong, fair or unfair. Another characteristic of this type of black-and-white thinking is the presence of rigid rules. There is a correct way to do things, and it is upsetting when things are not done correctly. In addition, there are often many things that "should" or "must" or "can't" be done by oneself or others.

2. High Level of Creativity:

People suffering from severe anxiety are usually very creative. Unfortunately, this creativity is the force behind two self-defeating activities. The first, negative anticipation or "what if" thinking, is the tendency to think of frightening things that could occur in a given situation. The second is the tendency to vividly imagine these frightening possibilities. This is called awfulizing.

3. Excessive Need for Approval:

The excessive need for approval is often referred to as low self-esteem or self-acceptance. A person with this trait depends on others for a sense of self-worth. This creates a fear of rejection that results in a heightened sensitivity to criticism and difficulty in saying "no" to the demands of others. An excessive need for approval can also create the tendency to take responsibility for the feelings of others and to be overly sensitive to other's needs.

4. Perfectionism

Perfectionism is the tendency to use all-or-nothing thinking when evaluating one's actions. Along with this black-and-white thinking there is usually a tendency to focus on achievement. These two traits cause the perfectionist to consider any less-than-perfect achievement as a failure which is personalized so that both the task and the person become failures.

5. Extremely High Expectations of Self

The combination of perfectionism, rigid thinking, and excessive need for approval creates the expectation from oneself of a much higher level of performance and accomplishment than would ever be expected from others.

6. Competent, Dependable "Doer"

The interaction of all the above creates a person who is not only competent, capable and dependable, but also one who is a real "doer." He/she is skilled at getting jobs done well and always expects this of his or herself.

7. Excessive Need to be in Control

A person with this trait will often place a high value on being calm and in control. Often there is a need for events to be predictable. Unexpected changes in a predetermined schedule may cause distress because it is harder to be in control when one is not sure what will happen. There may also be a tendency to try to control the feelings and behavior of others, but out of fear of losing control. A person with the need to be in control can often experience intense anxiety symptoms yet appear normal to the casual observer. A person like this usually presents a "proper" image to others. It is their responsibility to keep others happy in the world even when there is tremendous turmoil inside. He or she may be considered to be very strong by friends and family.

8. Suppression of Negative Feelings

A person with the above traits often suppress feelings that "shouldn't" be felt because they might cause a loss of control or experience disapproval from friends or relatives.

9. Ignoring the Body's Physical Needs

This trait is commonly reflected in the attitude that the body is unimportant. Signs from the body indicating it is tired or in pain tend to be ignored or given a low priority. A person with this trait is frequently only aware of fatigue when the symptoms of exhaustion is present.

* Adapted from Anxiety, Phobias & Panic by Reneau Peurfoy

The Impact of Stress:

Stress can have a profound impact on people, affecting them in various ways.

Generalized stress is a state where someone is constantly overwhelmed by excessive worry, remains on edge continually, struggles with sleep, and finds it difficult to experience pleasure and relaxation.

Post-Traumatic Stress, on the other hand, occurs when an individual has endured a traumatic, life-threatening event. They may continue to experience severe stress, nightmares, hyper-vigilance, avoidance of similar situations, and angry outbursts for months or even years afterward.

Phobias represent intense fears that emerge when a person is exposed to specific situations or stimuli, such as darkness, heights, snakes, the sight of blood, or certain social situations like public speaking. Obsessive-Compulsive Reactions develop as a response to stress or chaos in one's life, leading a person to engage in repetitive thinking and worrying about something, known as obsessions, or to perform repetitive behaviors like excessive handwashing or constant checking, referred to as compulsions.

Panic Attacks are among the most debilitating manifestations of stress. These sudden, intense episodes seem to come out of nowhere, striking even when there is no apparent danger. They typically last for a few minutes before subsiding. During a panic attack, the person may experience chest pains, a sensation of suffocation, dizziness, rapid heartbeats, profuse sweating, numbness, or nausea. These physical symptoms can be accompanied by intense fears of death, going insane, or losing control. Those who suffer from panic attacks often live in constant fear of the next episode, which may prevent them from leaving their homes, being alone, or driving.

Managing Stress*

All of us experience stress, to one degree or another, in our everyday lives. Stress is the body's reaction to an event that is experienced as disturbing or threatening. Our primitive ancestors experienced stress when they had to fight off wild animals and other threats. In the contemporary world we are more likely to experience stress when we face overwhelming responsibilities at work or home, experience loneliness, or fear losing things which are important to us, such as our jobs or friends. When we are exposed to such an event, we experience what has been called the "fight or flight" response. To prepare for fighting or fleeing, the body increases its heart rate and blood pressure. This sends more blood to our heart and muscles, and our respiration rate increases. Some stress is positive is positive when it prompts us to act to solve a problem. Public speakers, athletes, and entertainers have long known that stress can be used to energize themselves and their presentations.

The Power of Stress: A Positive Force for Actors and Public Speakers

Stress is often viewed as a negative force that can have detrimental effects on one's health and well-being. However, for actors and public speakers, stress can be a powerful tool when harnessed effectively. I want to explore, with you, the positive effects of stress in these professions and how it can contribute to peak performance, authenticity, and compelling communication. If they can use stress to enhance their performance we can do the same. Part of conquering stress is using its positive aspects Actors and public speakers often find themselves in high-pressure situations, such as live performances or addressing large audiences. Stress, when managed appropriately, can act as a performance enhancer. The adrenaline rush associated with stress can sharpen focus, increase energy levels, and boost overall performance. This heightened state of alertness can lead to more dynamic and engaging presentations.

Stressful situations can evoke genuine emotions, and for actors, this authenticity is crucial for delivering a convincing performance. The emotional intensity brought about by stress allows actors to tap into a wider range of emotions, bringing depth and realism to their characters. Similarly, public speakers can use stress to connect with their audience on a more emotional level, making their message more relatable and impactful.

Stressful situations often require quick thinking and adaptability. Actors thrive on the unexpected challenges that stress can introduce during live performances. Public speakers, when faced with unexpected hurdles, can use stress as a catalyst for creative problem-solving and improvisation. This ability to think on their feet can elevate both the performance and the message being delivered.

Regular exposure to stress can contribute to the development of resilience. Actors and public speakers who navigate and overcome challenging situations become more resilient in the face of adversity. Overcoming stressors can boost self-confidence and self-efficacy, leading to a positive cycle where individuals become more capable and composed in the face of future challenges.

Stress can create vulnerability, and when managed effectively, this vulnerability can be a powerful tool for building a connection with the audience. Both actors and public speakers can use their shared humanity, including the experience of stress, to create a genuine connection with their audience. This shared emotional experience can make the performance or presentation more memorable and impactful.

While stress is often portrayed negatively, for actors and public speakers, it can be a catalyst for enhanced performance, authenticity, and connection. By understanding how to harness stress as a positive force, individuals in these professions can turn pressure into an ally, using it to deliver compelling and memorable experiences for their audiences.

* Adapted from *Stress Can Help Us Convert Problems into Solutions Emotional Wellness Matters*, by Robert B Simmonds, Ph.D. * www.emotionalwellness.com

Whenwearestressedwebecomevigilantandtense.Ourbodiesenduponfull alert. We can use our perceived stress as a clue. In fact, seeing that there is a problem and that we need to solve it, can motivate us to perform much better. The real difficulty occurs when we feel blocked. For various reasons, we may be unable to solve the problem — perhaps because we don't realize that there is a problem, or we don't have the tools for solving it — and we continue to expose ourselves to the stress. In such instances, stress becomes a negative experience. Negative stress is demanding on our bodies and our lives in general. When our bodies are in a constant state of readiness for prolonged periods of time, we end up with heart palpitations, increased blood pressure, sweating, high stomach acidity, stomach spasms, and muscle spasms.

There is evidence that prolonged stress can lead to heart disease and a compromised immune system. Stress can deplete our energy and interfere with our concentration. It can lead us to become abrupt with other people and to engage in emotional outbursts or even physical violence. Our relationships and job security can be jeopardized. People who experience unresolved stress are more prone to self-destructive behaviors such as drug and alcohol abuse.

Those who deal with stress in a positive way usually have:

- a sense of ***self-determination***
- a feeling of ***involvement in life's experiences***, and
- an ability to change negatives into ***positives***. Making lemonade out of lemons.

Self-determination refers to an ability to control or adapt to the events of everyday living. Rather than seeing ourselves as helpless in trying to overcome obstacles, we can begin to define ourselves as problem-solvers. We can remember times when we have been successful in solving problems and then see ourselves in those terms. We can learn to trust that we will have success in meeting life's difficulties. When we take this approach, we can begin to face problematic situations as a challenge which, when resolved, can bring new and exciting opportunities into our lives.

Involvement means opening ourselves up to the world around us. It means letting friends and family members into our personal lives and sharing our private experiences with others when appropriate. Cultivating a social network serves us well when we are dealing with stressful situations. Talking our way through a crisis in the presence of a supportive listener, rather than holding it in alone, is one of our best ways of gaining helpful feedback, putting the situation into perspective, and sensing that we are not alone. When we lack involvement with others, we often feel vulnerable and may question whether we have the resources to cope with stressful experiences.

A positive approach toward life is one of the main attributes of those who deal well with stress. Rather than seeing life's difficulties as situations to complain about, the more adaptive person sees them as challenges which can be met with success. Losses can be seen as opportunities for gain. The life process is one of loss and gain — it's as natural as night and day. When we trust that our losses will give rise to new gains and life experiences, the stress associated with loss need not be devastating. For example, the loss of a job opens the door to more satisfying employment and the opportunity for more fulfilling life experiences.

The clue is to change our negative thoughts about situations into more positive thoughts — and positive *feelings* will usually follow a change in thinking. Another example, is a close friend moves away, rather than harboring negative thoughts about how lonely and devastated you will feel, think about the good memories you will always have, how your friendship will leave a positive legacy that will always touch your life, how you can keep in touch and visit, and how you can now spend your time in new and positive pursuits. There really is no need for stress.

In this situation, we can choose to move toward the open doors of life rather than futilely knocking on closed doors. The clue to handling stress adaptively is to acquire the skills we need to feel empowered. This requires a good, honest exploration into our lives. We need to explore the strengths that we already have for coping with stress, as well as to learn new skills. We need to be able both to comfort ourselves and to let others nurture us as well. All of us can learn, with some healthy exploration, to conquer our stress.

The Top Life Stressors:

Researchers have identified several life stressors which are associated with vulnerability to anxiety, accidents, and physical problems. Here are the top fifteen on the list, along with a rating which indicates the severity of stress associated with each of these life events. The higher the number, the more likely a person will be prone to stress related problems. Even good events, like marriage, can bring on stress.

TOP LIFE
STRESSORS
(Higher the number, the more likely a person
will be prone to stress related problems)
100
Death of a
Spouse
73
Divorce
65
Marital
Separation
63
Detention
in jail or other
institution
63
Death of
close family
member
53
Major personal
injury or
illness
50
Marriage
47
Being fired
at work
45
Marital
reconciliation
45
Retirement
from work
44
family member
health change
40
Pregnancy
39
Sexual
difficulties
39
Major business
readjustment

Some Proven Ways to Cope with Stress:

The first step is to increase your level of awareness in two areas — first, your level of how you experience stress in your body, and second, the type of the events which bring on, or trigger your stress. You need to do the first one before you can effectively do the second. To increase your level of awareness in your body, check your stress levels throughout the day and rate yourself, perhaps on a ten-point scale, on the degree of stress you are experiencing at that time. To do this, check out your body. Are your muscles tense? Is your heart pounding? Are your hands cold and clammy? Are you able to concentrate normally? When you become good at recognizing the degree of stress you are currently experiencing, work on increasing your awareness of the people, things and events that are triggering your stress. These can also be rated on a ten-point scale. This exercise can yield a lot of surprises. For example, you might find that a close friend, a family member or your job may increase your stress levels dramatically. You may learn to avoid the stressors or else to deal with them more realistically. Doing this exercise within the context of managing your mind may lead you to explore life issues which can finally be resolved. The second step in learning to deal with stress is to take positive action to reduce your Internal and external tension. Incorporating the following techniques can serve as an effective tool for combating unnecessary stress, and they may even change how you live your daily life.

Put the basic systems of life in place: Eat healthy, sleep well, and drink water. In addition, make sure the following are part of your lifestyle:

Relaxation: There is a wide range of relaxation techniques available for coping with stress. Most of these methods can be easily learned, but the most important point to keep in mind is that you should find techniques that work for you. The list of choices includes breathing exercises, yoga, stretching exercises, biofeedback, meditation, massage, visual imagery, and progressive muscle relaxation.

Exercise: Regular physical exercise helps reduce stress, and it also raises self- esteem. It primes your immune system and plays a crucial role in preventing disease.

Physical exercise need not be strenuous. Walking at a brisk pace for 20 or 30 minutes daily decreases stress just as effectively as vigorous jogging.

Self-Rejuvenation: Find things you enjoy that make your spirit soar. This could include listening to music, meditation, prayer, sports, dance, painting, visiting nature, hiking, or writing. Take time for recreational and spiritual pursuits on a regular basis.

This will help you to maintain balance and perspective in your life - and it gives you better management over being stressed out.

Setting Limits: Much stress, especially these days, comes from biting off more than we can chew. We often embrace faulty expectations about how much we should accomplish in life. Unfortunately, this is a prime culprit in increasing our stress levels. It may help to examine what is really important in our lives, scale back, think smaller, and give our time more completely to the things that matter the most. Bringing expectations into line with reality and learning to say no when we choose to offer immediate relief.

Effective Communication: If you are too passive with others, you may come to feel that everyone is taking advantage of you or controlling you. On the other hand, if you are too aggressive in your dealings with other people, you may antagonize them and create more stress for yourself. Communication training is one way of expressing your needs without feeling ignored or offending others.

Several effective communication techniques can be explored and learned.

There are two skills:
   A. Effective Speaking:

1.   **Non-verbal's Honesty words match actions**
2.   **Validation Empathy**
3.   **Speak from your heart**
4.   **Express respect and warmth**
5.   **Speak from feeling and experience rather than theory or opinion.**

6. **Share your feelings or ideas directly, telling others how you are experiencing them.**

   B. Active Listening:

1. **Paraphrase what another has said to make sure you understand.**
2. **Listen with sensitivity and show concern for feelings expressed verbally and non-verbally.**
3. **Encourage another to speak when he/she seems to have something to share and respect silence when they prefer not to share. Practice sharing yourself.**

Social Support: Find people who can nurture and support you and learn to trust appropriately in them. Our stress levels increase when we try to deal with life's difficulties alone. Talking things through with a good listener can help us to put things into a more realistic perspective — and the mere act of talking about issues that we usually hold inside serves to reduce our stress levels. We can take charge of our lives in an effective way — and this is a much better alternative than living under the control of stress.

Add Meditation and Self Hypnosis and you have a dynamite plan to manage stress!

Meditation Made Easy

1. **Grounding:** Relax your body, clear your mind. Run roots into the earth and drain negative energy and purify. Bring energy back up into your body.

2. **Mindfulness:** Sit in a comfortable relaxed position. You can sit either on the floor with your legs crossed or in a chair. Rest your hands lightly on your thighs with the palms down. Cast your eyes down but leave them slightly open. Focus your attention on your breath. Breathe deeply rhythmically. Quiet your mind by focusing on your breath znd consciously putting your thoughts away. As thoughts appear, bring your attention gently back to your breath. After your period of open-eyed mindfulness, close your eyes and visualize having a wonderful day or achieving a goal. Key elements are to use the breath and body to stay present in the here and now. Practice for at least 10 minutes 2 X a day. Work up to 20 minutes. 2 X a day.

Benefits:

1. **Improves ability to handle stress.**
2. **Increases retention of information/improves memory**

3. **Gives emotional space. Allows you to handle emotions better.**
4. **Cuts down on reactivity and triggering.**
5. **Improves concentration and focus.**
6. **Supports immune system functioning and body's ability to handle disease.**

Three Minute Vacation: Sit in a comfortable relaxed position. You can sit either on the floor with your legs crossed or in a chair. Rest your hands lightly on your thighs with the palms down. Close your eyes and visualize having a wonderful vacation. Count 300 breaths. Do these 3 to 5 times a day. Copy this link I your browser and download a great MP 3 that is a great addition to Help you conquer stress http://zoilitagrant.net/media/files/03Stress_Free/dlcd03.htm

IMAGINE YOU ARE IN CHARGE OF YOUR LIFE!

Guess What You Are? There is Magic in Your Mind.

ELIMINATING ANXIETY

Anxiety makes everything worse. It spins your mind around in circles, activates negative thoughts, and interference with sleep. It makes it harder to enjoy life and practice the skills of successful living. It is the first symptom of stress overload. The second is depression. For many people life becomes a teetertotter of anxiety followed by bouts of depression.

Anxiety, is a very strong emotional state, not only making your life challenges seem worse, it also engulfs your mind in a relentless cycle of negative thoughts, creating hurdles in achieving restful sleep. Beyond its immediate impact, anxiety serves as a precursor to stress overload, acting as the initial warning signal. This stress overload, when left unaddressed, can escalate to a second, more crippling symptom: depression.

The intertwining of anxiety and depression forms a complex dynamic, transforming your experience of life into a precarious balance, akin to a teetertotter. The oscillation between heightened anxiety and episodes of profound melancholy becomes a defining feature for many individuals navigating the intricate terrain of mental well-being. This intricate interplay underscores the challenges of maintaining successful living skills, emphasizing the importance of addressing anxiety as a crucial step in preventing its effects on your life.

Many people try to find balance through caffeine and sugar contributing to obesity and many health conditions. According to the Center for Disease Control more people are taking drugs for anxiety and insomnia than ever before. and eleven **percent of Americans aged 12 years and over, take antidepressant medication d**esigned in a large part to manage anxiety. There has got to be a better way! I am here to tell you there is. Learn to use the power your mind. It is the better way.

Let me tell you a story about a man named Ben. Ben was a very likeable guy.

He worked hard in both his work and personal life. His marriage was good, his nearly grown son and daughter were doing well. One day Ben and his family decided to drive to the top of Pike's Peak in Colorado. This is a majestic Colorado mountain so grand in scale but is also accessible to experience first-hand by people of all ages and abilities by this highway. The safe and scenic Pikes Peak Highway provides people the opportunity to enjoy 19 miles of mountain terrain. It was a hot day in July, the highway was crowed, and Ben began to have car trouble almost immediately. He pulled over a few times to let honking drivers pass. Finally, about three quarters of the way up the mountain Ben's car died. There was nowhere to pull over. It was hot and impatient drivers were honking wildly. Ben's wife was telling him to pull over and he was getting upset.

Ben had his first, full blown and intense panic attack. Both Ben and

Helen, his wife thought it was a heart attack. Helen called 911. Other drivers tried to pass. Emergency vehicles jammed the other lane and the situation slipped into chaos. By the time Ben reached the emergency room, his blood pressure was sky high, his heart rate was way too fast and he was having trouble breathing. They kept him in the hospital overnight doing numerous tests and releasing him the next day with recommendations to go anti-anxiety medication. He went on the medication which created digestive problems and interfered with his sleep. He added two more medications and felt horrible most of the time. And he kept having panic attacks. Now he was having them every time he got highly stressed. Finally, Helen said, "There has got to be a better way"!

Then they came to see me. By learning to use the power his mind, Ben eliminated his anxiety and stopped his panic attacks. Mindpower is the better way. After the first panic attack, Ben developed consistent negative self-talk. He was constantly criticizing himself. That was the first thing to change. We created a Self-Talk Menu for Ben to work with.

Self-Suggestion and Self Talk

This created positive statements for Ben to use in working through his feelings about his anxiety and symptoms, it produced. I taught him to meditate and utilize trance to teach positive self-talk he practiced in self-hypnosis. He used these suggestions as he talked to himself throughout the day. Suggestion like "perhaps you have suffered enough" was very helpful. "I can manage this / I can handle it." "I am a lot more than my anxiety." "This condition / illness is not my fault / I am not to blame!" All these statements became a part of Ben's self-talk. When creating your menu consider these:

Areas to Develop Self Talk About

1. **Emotions**
    A. Depression
    B. Anxiety
    C. Fears

2. **Patterns established in childhood.**
   A. Ethnic traditions
   B. Role models being copied.
3. **Characteristics**
   A. Low motivation
   B. Poor Self Image
   C. Lack of pride in accomplishments

Ben and I worked together for more than a year as he eliminated his lifelong anxiety. Along the way he not only stopped his panic attacks, cured his insomnia, lowered his blood pressure, he also lost nearly 25 pounds. He also helped me to remember that when people are taught to change the way, they think they can dramatically improve their health and quality of life. This is probably where I got the idea for my online **Breakthrough to Brilliance** program.

Effects of Traumatic Experiences*.

We live in a world that is very traumatizing. Between political divide and constant violence many people feel unsafe and in danger. When people feel themselves in danger, they are overcome with feelings of fear, helplessness, and extreme anxiety. Traumatic experiences become part of everyday life for many. Some common traumatic experiences include being physically attacked, being in a serious accident, being in combat, being sexually assaulted, being exposed to mass shootings and being in a fire or a disaster like a hurricane or a tornado. Even watching violence in movies, TV, and video games can feel traumatic. After traumatic experiences, people are usually extremely anxious and may have problems that they didn't have before the event. Anxiety becomes free floating and can last for years.

How Traumatic Experiences Affect People

People who go through traumatic experiences often have symptoms and problems afterward. How serious the symptoms and problems are depends on many things including a person's life experiences before the trauma, a person's own natural ability to cope with stress, how serious the trauma was, and what kind of help and support a person gets from family, friends, and professionals immediately following the trauma.

Because most people are not familiar with how trauma affects people, they often have trouble understanding what is happening to them and this increases their anxiety. They may think the trauma is their fault, that they are going crazy, or that there is something wrong with them because other people who experienced the trauma don't appear to have the same problems. They may turn to drugs or alcohol to make themselves feel better. They may turn away from friends and family who don't seem to understand. They may not know what to do to get better. Their anxiety becomes overwhelming

What You Need to Know Coping with Trauma

1. Traumas happen to many competent, healthy, strong, good people.
2. No one can completely protect himself or herself from traumatic experiences.
3. Many people have long-lasting problems following exposure to trauma. Up to 8% of individuals will have PTSD at some time in their lives.
4. People who react to trauma are not going crazy. They are experiencing symptoms and problems that relate to having been in a traumatic situation. Many people experience some degree of trauma in their everyday lives and many more carry scars from their childhood. Having symptoms after a traumatic event is not a sign of personal weakness. Many psychologically well-adjusted and physically healthy people develop anxiety because of being traumatized by something in the past. Probably everyone would develop PTSD if they were exposed to a severe enough trauma. When a person understands trauma symptoms better, they can become less fearful of them and better able to manage the increased anxiety.

What are the common effects of trauma?

In the aftermath of a traumatic event, individuals frequently find themselves engulfed by an intense and paralyzing sense of fear. After the occurrence, reactions unfold as they feel a pervasive re-experiencing of the trauma, both in their mental and physical bodies. This re-experiences presents as distressing memories, which can manifest as vivid images or persistent thoughts that intrusively infiltrate their consciousness, perpetuating the emotional and psychological impact of the traumatic event.

Moreover, the re-experiencing of trauma often extends beyond mere recollections. Individuals may encounter flashbacks, wherein they feel as though they are reliving the traumatic incident, complete with the accompanying emotional and sensory elements. These flashbacks can be triggered by seemingly innocuous stimuli, creating a heightened state of vulnerability and emotional turbulence for those affected.

Additionally, the aftermath of trauma may give rise to a heightened state of hypervigilance, where individuals become hyper-alert and sensitive to potential threats in their environment. This heightened arousal can lead to difficulties in concentration, sleep disturbances, and a pervasive sense of unease, further complicating the process of recovery.

Understanding the multifaceted nature of trauma and its aftermath is crucial for devising comprehensive support systems and interventions aimed at alleviating the enduring effects on individuals' mental and emotional well-being.

People may experience the following:

- **Feeling as if the trauma is happening again (flashbacks)**
- **Bad dreams and nightmares**
- **Getting upset when reminded about the trauma (by something the person sees, hears, feels, smells, or tastes)**
- **Anxiety or fear, feeling in danger again.**
- **Anger or aggressive feelings and feeling the need to defend oneself.**
- **Trouble managing emotions because reminders lead to sudden anxiety, anger, or upset.**
- **Trouble concentrating or thinking clearly.**
- **Trouble falling or staying asleep.**
- **Feeling agitated and constantly on the lookout for danger.**

- **Getting very startled by loud noises or something or someone coming up on you from behind when you don't expect it.**
- **Feeling shaky and sweaty.**
- **Having your heart pound or having trouble breathing.**

Avoidance Symptoms

Because thinking about the trauma and feeling as if you are in danger is upsetting, people who have been through traumas often try to avoid reminders of the trauma.

Sometimes people are aware that they are avoiding reminders, but other times they do not realize that their behavior is motivated by the need to avoid reminders of the trauma.

Ways of avoiding thoughts, feelings, and sensations associated with the trauma can include:

- Actively avoiding trauma-related thoughts and memories.
- Avoiding conversations and staying away from places, activities, or people that might remind you of the trauma.
- Trouble remembering important parts of what happened during the trauma
- Shutting down emotionally or feeling emotionally numb
- Trouble having loving feelings or feeling any strong emotions
- Feeling disconnected from the world around you and things that happen to you
- Avoiding situations that might make you have a strong emotional reaction
- Feeling weird physical

(*Adapted from a National Center for PTSD Fact Sheet by Eve B. Carlson, Ph.D. and Josef Ruzek, Ph.D.)

Constant anxiety becomes the norm. There has got to be a better way. There is. Learn to use the power of your mind.

Starfish Breathing

This is simple, easy, and effective. Stretch one hand out like a big star fish. Then take a finger from you other hand and trace around your outstretched fingers….breathing in from the nose and out from the mouth. Do these 3 to 5 times and watch your anxiety fade!

Remember this list:

Characteristics of a High Anxiety Personality
  Rigid Thinking
1. **High Level of Creativity**
2. **Excessive Need for Approval**
3. **Perfectionism**
4. **Extremely High Expectations of Self**
5. **Competent, Dependable "Doer"**
6. **Excessive Need to be in Control**
7. **Suppression of Negative Feelings**
8. **Ignoring the Body's Physical Needs**

When Debbie first came to see me, she could check off most of these. She was a single mom with two girls ages nine, and eleven. She was working 40 hours a week as a receptionist at a busy dental office. She was making $30,000 a year and described herself as over worked, under paid, and wanting a better way to live. She felt consumed with anxiety and worry. Debbie's early life had its share of trauma with her parents' contentious divorce. Things were so bad that her parents had to meet at the police station to exchange Debbie and her younger brother. Debbie had been anxious from her early childhood. Her anxiety started the pattern of constant worrying. The worrying kept her up at night and interfered with her ability to be happy. Stopping the worrying was our first goal.

How to Stop Worrying*

  Attack the challenge, rather than letting it attack you.
  Attack the challenge, rather than letting it attack you.

- **Analyze the problem and take corrective action**. This is what non-worriers do. Sit down with a spouse or friend and ask, "What concrete corrective action can I take to reduce my worries on this matter?" It is better to do this with someone—because alone you'll be more likely to become anxious and quit.
- **Exercise at least every other day.** Exercise helps prevent toxic worry. It reduces the background noise or anxiety the brain accumulates during the average day.
- **Develop connectedness** in as many ways as you can. Whether it is feeling connected to your family, or the connections with people we have from our past, or our connections to friends, neighbors and colleagues, or our feelings of belonging to the people we work, play or learn with, or the connectedness we feel being a part of nature, or feeling held in the hands of the Divine. The more you develop and increase your feelings of connectedness, the less you will suffer from toxic kinds of worry.
- **Attack your worry**; don't let it attack you. Charge toward the issue. Then you will not over think the problem of how to handle it instead.

Pray or meditate. If you are spiritual, pray every day. This is good for your soul, and it can make you worry less. Learn to meditate. Practice the techniques of Meditation Made Easy. Prayer and meditation help us keep things in perspective. They calm our minds.

- **Add structure to your life**. Many everyday worries are directly related to disorganization: What have I forgotten? Why didn't I bring that brochure with me? Lists, reminders, a daily schedule, a basket next to the front door where you always put your car keys so you don't start off your day with a frantic search for your keys—these concrete bits of structure can dramatically reduce the amount of time you spend each day in useless or destructive worry.

Try doing something that you like. It is almost impossible to worry destructively if you are engaged in a task you enjoy. More than anything turns off you gloom-and-doom generator!

*Adapted from Worry by Edward M. Hallowell

*People who are problem-worriers have a tendency to "catastrophize" ordinary circumstances. They can turn a minor problem into a potential disaster. By awfulizing and pumping up everyday worries into possible catastrophes the worrier inflicts p*ain upon themselves. Never worry alone. When you share a worry, the worry almost always diminishes. You often find solutions to a problem when you talk it out, and the mere fact of putting it into words takes it out of the threatening realm of the imagination—and into a more concrete manageable form.

Look for what is good in life. We are reminded so often of what is bad that. we must look for what is good. Take an inventory everyday of what is good.

Big things—children, friends, health, a mate—and little things. Every day, before you go to sleep, look at what you are grateful for.

Tips to Reduce Anxiety

Anxiety is a common and normal human experience, but it can become overwhelming. Anxiety can significantly interfere with daily life in various ways, impacting a person's emotional, cognitive, and physical well-being. Here are some common ways in which anxiety can affect daily functioning:

1. **Difficulty concentrating**-Anxiety often leads to racing thoughts and an inability to focus on tasks, making it challenging to concentrate on work or daily activities.
2. **Memory problems**-High levels of anxiety can affect memory, leading to forgetfulness and difficulty recalling information.
3. **Mood swings**-Anxiety can cause mood swings, leading to irritability, frustration, and emotional instability.
4. **Fears and Worries**-Excessive worry about future events or perceived threats can dominate a person's thoughts, making it difficult to enjoy the present moment.
5. **Relationship problems**-Anxiety can strain relationships as the constant worry and fear may affect communication and interpersonal dynamics.
6. **Sleep disturbances** Anxiety can lead to difficulty falling asleep or staying asleep, resulting in fatigue and decreased energy levels.
7. Physical problems Physical symptoms such as muscle tension, headaches, and stomachaches are common. Anxiety activates the body's "fight or flight" response, leading to increased heart rate and rapid breathing, which can be uncomfortable and contribute to feelings of unease.
8. **Decision making** Anxiety can lead to overthinking and excessive worry about making the wrong decisions, making it challenging to make choices confidently. Anxiety may contribute to a fear of failure, causing individuals to avoid taking risks or trying new things.
9. **Chronic anxiety** may weaken the immune system over time, making individuals more susceptible to illnesses.

It's important to note that anxiety exists on a spectrum, and its impact can vary from person to person. Some people feel anxious only sometimes, while others might feel it a lot. For some, anxiety may be a normal response to stress, while for others, it can be a chronic and debilitating condition requiring professional intervention. Most anxiety can be managed by your mind.

Here are some tips to reduce anxiety:

Practice relaxation techniques: Deep breathing exercises, meditation, yoga, and progressive muscle relaxation can help to calm the mind and body.

1. **Stay active**: Engage in regular exercise or physical activity to release endorphins and reduce stress hormones.
2. **Get enough sleep**: Aim for 8-9 hours of sleep each night to help your body and mind recharge.
3. **Eat a healthy diet**: A well-balanced diet that includes plenty of fruits, vegetables, lean proteins, and whole grains can help to regulate mood and reduce anxiety.
4. **Limit caffeine and alcohol**: These substances can exacerbate anxiety symptoms and interfere with sleep.
5. **Practice self-care**: Make time for activities that you enjoy, such as reading, taking a bath, or spending time outdoors.
6. **Challenge negative thoughts**: Anxiety often stems from negative or distorted thinking patterns. Challenge these thoughts by questioning their validity and replacing them with more positive and realistic thoughts.
7. **Seek support**: Don't hesitate to reach out to friends, family, or a mental health professional for support and guidance.

Debbie was so successful in managing her own anxiety she decided to change careers and help others. She studied with me and became a hypnotic coach. Being a hypnotic life coach has made her an expert in working to eliminate anxiety and achieving lasting weight mastery. She has high paying clients who refer friends. As a single Mom, Debbie has time to be with her kids and money to live comfortably.

She now works 20 hours a week, makes $80,000 a year and more time to spend with her girls. She changed her mind and changed her life!

CHAPTER 3

LIFTING DEPRESSION

Depression is a far more common emotional disability than most people realize. It is estimated that as much as half the population experiences a period of depression during their lifetime and that at any given time, as many as eight million people in the United States need of help to lift their depression. Many people that they are living lives of quiet desperation. They don't realize they are depressed and deal with their moods with caffeine and sugar.

Depression goes undetected largely for two reasons. First, there is a stigma attached to depression. For many people, it indicates a sign of serious mental illness or weakness. This was particularly evident during the 1972 presidential campaign when the Democratic Vice-Presidential candidate, Thomas Eagleton, revealed he had been treated for depression. Even though he had recovered, he was forced to drop out because of adverse public opinion. That stigma still exists today.

The second reason that depression often goes undetected is because the condition is often interpreted as unhappiness or sadness. Feeling sad does not carry the fear of serious emotional problems and therefore is a more acceptable view for many people. As a result, many people live lives of constant low-level sadness. There has got to be a better way. There is. You can use the power of your mind to lift your depression and live a more satisfying life. I want to help you do it.

What then is depression? Webster defines depression as "low spirits; dejection." Other dictionary definitions also contribute to an understanding of the word—"a hollow or low place; a decrease of force." Symptoms include difficulty sleeping, lowering of spirits, loss of self-esteem, loss of perspective, fatigue, loss of energy, a desire to avoid other people, reduced sexual desire and ability, increase, or decrease in appetite, weight loss or gain, a feeling of being trapped, difficulty making decisions, hypersensitivity, many fears, irritability, and unfounded physical complaints.

Depression is overload of stress resulting from emotional burnout, trauma, or loss. Clinically speaking, depression falls into two categories: acute and chronic. The symptoms of each are similar. Acute depression is short term, sometimes lasting a few days, but generally ending within a few weeks or months. It is intense, painful, and attached to a particular event such as the death of a loved one, an ended relationship or job loss. It may also be triggered by stressful events or changes, positive or negative. It is an experience of loss with an appropriate duration for the event that triggers it. The overall intensity of acute depression will vary depending upon childhood experiences that are connected through an emotional, similar experience. Acute depression is an outlet for strong feelings that offer the individual an opportunity to gain new insights.

Chronic depression is long term and usually disabling and includes an immobilizing quality. This immobilization tends to prevent the sufferer from being able to perform the kinds of activities that lead one out of depression. Although the general signs are like acute depression, the chronic condition is often more difficult to identify because of its long-term and more subtle qualities. Often a person with chronic depression is seen as a pessimist or worrier. The direct cause of the chronic depression is often not connected to their life.

People tend to store their emotions in the subconscious. Unexperienced feelings from an earlier time in your life are often the foundation of chronic depression. Exploring the unfamiliar emotions that were created in earlier phases of your life can frequently serve as the tool for letting go of their impact on you. These feelings are stuck and serve as one of the causes for the development of chronic depression. These uncharted feelings, often stemming from formative experiences and unresolved issues, may become ingrained in your subconscious emotional landscape, contributing significantly to the persistence of depressive states over time. It is crucial to recognize and let go of these historical emotional undercurrents to foster a more comprehensive understanding of the roots of chronic depression and work towards effective strategies for healing and resilience. I have seen that these old feelings can be released eliminating much depression.

A young lady, named Amanda once said to me, "I have everything in life to be happy: a loving marriage, healthy children, and work part time at a job I love. I am still sad all the time!" She was carrying sadness of her childhood. All her life she had pushed down feelings. She had never really let go of that sadness. Working with her mind, she was able in a few months to let go of pain of her inner child and become a happy empowered adult woman.

Warning Signs of Depression

- Unwillingness to ask for things-Low self-confidence-Insecurity
- Destructive risk-taking Suicidal thoughts
- Paranoia
- Unable to experience pleasure
- Hard to get up in the morning
- Poor judgement
- Obsessive thought
- Repeated words/actions Procrastination
- Negative attitude
- Unable to concentrate.
- Difficulty exercising
- Difficulty completing normal daily tasks.

Physical Symptoms of Depression

- Hopeless Useless Apathetic
- Sad Abandoned Empty
- Guilty
- Scared
- Hate existence
- Ache all over
- Tight stomach Nausea
- Chest aches/Heart pain
- Constipation

- Jaws clenched
- Muscle spasms
- Headaches
- Backaches
- Heaviness of limbs
- Fainting spells
- No energy

Brandon had no idea he was depressed. He knew he was very sad and was not motivated. He had lost his job during the pandemic, broke up with his longtime girlfriend moved in with his parents. He felt that he had hit bottom and that his life was over. He let his hair and beard grow and live in sweat clothes. He had constant headaches and stomach problems. He quit eating with his parents and spent hours smoking marijuana and playing video games. He refused to do therapy. He had done it in the past and did not feel it had helped. Same thing with medication. "Been there and done that" was his answer. He had met me in a social situation and was willing to try coaching with me.

Since he was fascinated with hypnosis, I started teaching him self-hypnosis. This is a perfect tool to lift depression. He started replacing his marijuana use with hypnosis MP3 and using self-hypnosis to increase his motivation. He realized that the restaurant job he had lost was not really what he wanted to do with his life. We began to talk about going to college and with his parents support he enrolled at local junior college. He developed inner guidance by learning to use his own intuition. Emotional clearing techniques removed the pain of the past.

We all have parts like a committee living inside our personality..... the judge, the rebel, and the child to name few. These parts act through emotions to influence our choices and our choices create our lives. I will go much further into this in the next chapters.

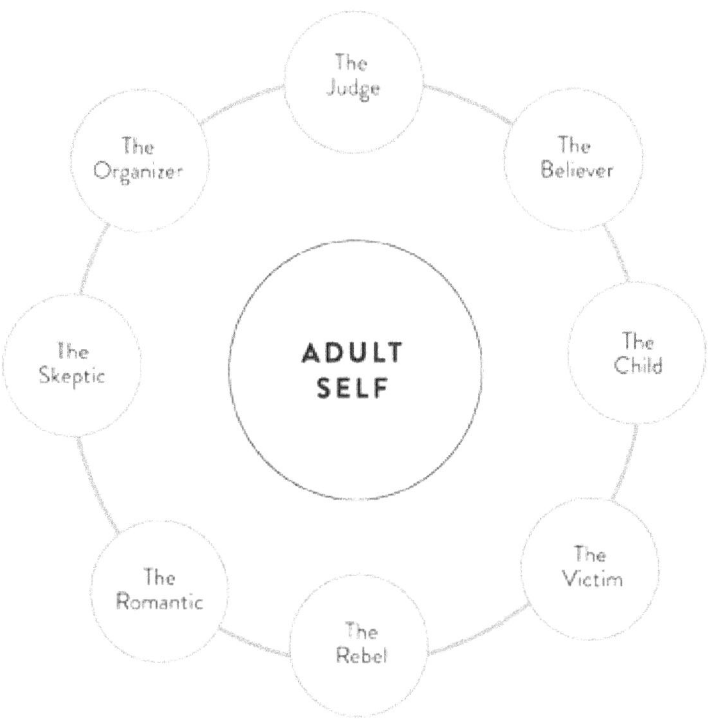

Brandon recently transferred from his junior college to a state university and is doing well in school. He changed his physical appearance. He cut his hair, changed out of sweats and has a smile on his face. He changed his mindset and now looks forward to the future. He used the power of his mind to get rid of his depression and reboot his life.

Common Feelings in Depression

- **Ugly**
- **Angry**
- **Helpless**
- **Failure**
- **Anxious**
- **Worthless**

- **Lonely**
- **Fearful**

Overcoming Fears

The main way to deal with fears and/or phobias is to use what we call desensitize.

This is done by creating a mental state safety and using that safety to eliminate the fear.

You focus on creating a safe place and a mental rehearsal of connecting your safe place with the action you fear.

Martha came to me depressed because she was afraid to fly. This prevented her from traveling with her husband on his business trips and was causing problems in her marriage. I used a desensitization experience with her. I had her create an imaginary safe place of personal power. Using a head nodding technique, I had her nod her head yes as soon as she experienced any fear with the imagery being used. When she nodded, I asked her to take a deep breath, focus on her safe and personal power place and as she exhaled to let the fear go, feeling calm, relaxed, and at peace. This would be repeated till the fear was released. I had her imagine calling the airline and choosing a flight best suited for her schedule, packing for the trip, checking baggage, waiting for boarding, entering the plane, taking off, flying to her destination, landing, and leaving the plane. At each step along the way, when she felt fear, she nodded yes. I told her to take a deep breath return to the safe place and blow out the fear, let the fear go: feel calm, relaxed, and at peace. We repeated this until she was able to go through the whole process of the event with feeling fear, focusing on her safe place, and releasing the fear. After two sessions she was able to easily fly. The power of her mind ended a problem she had had for years. She changed her mind and changed her life.

Types of Depression

Everyone feels sad from time to time. It's only natural. Most people go through blue days or normal periods of feeling down especially after they experience loss. But what specialists call clinical depression is different from just being "down in the dumps." The main difference is that the sad or empty mood does not go away after a couple of weeks and everyday activities like eating, sleeping, socializing, or working can be affected. Estimates indicate that perhaps one in five adults in the general population experiences a depressive disorder (e.g., major depression, bipolar disorder, dysthymia, postpartum depression, or seasonal affective disorder) at some point in their lives. In any given year over one in twenty people will have a depressive episode. For each person suffering directly from depression, three or four times that number (relatives, friends, associates) will also be affected to some degree. It is impossible to obtain exact figures because so many people try to live with this condition without looking for help. Recent studies strongly suggest that this condition is on the rise, especially among single women, women in poverty, single men, and adolescents. National tragedies or disasters can also generate depressive symptoms for large parts of the population.

A depressive disorder is known by a change a person's moods, thoughts, and feelings which are very negative. Without appropriate help, this condition can go on for a very long time: weeks, months, or years. Even among those suffering from depression, most do not even know they have the ability by using their mindpower to change their condition. Most blame themselves or may be blamed by others. This leads to alienation of family and friends who, if they knew of the illness, would likely offer support, and help find effective treatment. Although this is one of our most devastating emotional disorders, treatment can bring relief to over eighty percent of those who experience depression.

Several causes of depression have been identified. For example, the illness has been seen to run in families, suggesting that some people may have a genetic predisposition to depression, which may show itself particularly during times of stress. However, it is important to note that just because you have a family member with depression, you are not necessarily going to suffer from this condition yourself.

Sometimes a major change in a person's life patterns can trigger a depressive episode. These changes may be due to serious illness, a period of financial difficulties, stressful relationships, or a severe loss (such as a death of a loved one, divorce, or the loss of a job). Researchers find that people who are easily overwhelmed by stressful events, tend to worry, have low self-esteem, and see the world in a pessimistic way are prone to depression more than other people.

Not all people experience depressions the same way. The nature of one's depression depends on the cause and on each person's individual adaptation to this disorder. Here are several generally recognized forms of depression.

Major Depression

A major depression is different from a state of normal sadness. People who experience depression describe it as agonizing pain that cannot be shaken and seems to have no end in sight. They feel trapped and often talk about having a dark empty pit in their chest or stomach that cannot be filled. Some depressed people contemplate suicide. Virtually all people with depression complain about reduced energy, reduced ability to concentrate, and the inability to complete projects. About eighty percent of depressed people say they have trouble sleeping, with frequent nighttime awakening during which they worry about their problems. Many people with depression oversleep in the day- time. Many people with this disorder report that they have had either an increase or decrease in their appetite, sometimes accompanied by weight gain or weight loss. About fifty percent of people with depression say that their symptoms are worse in the morning and that they feel better by evening. Half of all people with depression report only one severe episode within their lifetimes, but the remainder may have this happen twice, or repeatedly, during their lives.

Symptoms of Major Depression

- **iminished ability to enjoy oneself.**
- **Loss of energy & interest.**
- **Difficulty concentrating; slowed and fuzzy thinking; indecision. – Magnified feelings of hopelessness, sadness, or anxiety.**
- **Decreased or increased sleep and/or appetite.**
- **Feelings of worthlessness or inappropriate guilt.**
- **Recurring thought of death.**

Adult Depression (Dysthymia)

Another common form of depressive disorder is called dysthymia. This involves having chronic, long-lasting symptoms of depression, which are not disabling, but prevent a person from functioning at top capacity or from feeling good. Women experience dysthymia about twice as often as men, and it is also found in those who lack a relationship and in those who are young or with few resources (such as a low income of few social contacts.) The primary symptoms include a depressed mood, a feeling of being down in the dumps, and a lack of interest in usual activities for at least two years. People with Dysthymia can experience any of the symptoms of major depression, but usually not to the severe degree that may be found in full blown depression. Dysthymic people, though, are vulnerable to moving into major depression during times of stress or crisis. Dysthymia often leads to a life without much pleasure, and many people with this condition feel that it is simply a part of their personality so that they never seek treatment.

Symptoms of Adult Depression include:

- **Poor appetite or overeating.**
- **Insomnia (lack of sleep) or hypersomnia (oversleeping) - low self-esteem**
- **Poor concentration or difficulty making decisions**
- **Feelings of hopelessness**
- **Fatigue or low energy.**

Bipolar Disorder

A third type of depressive disorder is bipolar disorder or manic-depressive illness. This disorder, which is much less common than major depression, is characterized by a pattern of cycling between periods of depression and elation. These cycles, or "mood swings," can be rapid, but most often occur gradually over time. When in the depressed part of the cycle, the person can experience any of the symptoms of depression. When the person moves into the manic or elated phase, however, he or she can experience irritability, severe insomnia, inappropriate social behavior (like going on spending sprees), talking rapidly with disconnected thoughts, increased energy, poor judgement and increased sexual desire.

There is strong evidence that bipolar disorder is largely an inherited condition, and many people with this disorder respond well to medication.

- **Symptoms of bipolar disorder are: high energy with a decreased need for sleep - extreme irritability rapid and unpredictable mood changes an exaggerated belief in one's abilities impulsive actions with damaging consequences (e.g., charging up credit cards, sudden love affairs, etc.)**

Post-Partum Depression

Post-Partum Depression (PPD) is primarily associated with the different hormonal shifts that occur in the after childbirth. It is a condition, characterized by a profound sense of sadness and emotional distress, can manifest as a severe form of depression, occasionally accompanied by psychotic features. However, it is noteworthy that most individuals grappling with this have positive responses to various treatment modalities.

The roots of post-partum depression come from the intricate interplay of hormonal fluctuations, psychological factors, and the challenges of adapting to the profound life changes that come with parenthood. While PPD can be a formidable adversary, it is essential to recognize that effective interventions, ranging from medication to wellness coaching, can significantly alleviate the symptoms.

Contrary to previous assumptions, post-partum depression is more prevalent than once believed, underscoring the importance of heightened awareness and support for new parents. By acknowledging the multifaceted nature of PPD, we can better comprehend its nuances, tailor treatments to individual needs, and foster a more empathetic and informed approach to addressing this common yet often underestimated mental health concern.

Seasonal Affective Disorder or **SAD**

Seasonal Affective Disorder (SAD) is a recurrent depressive condition that surfaces in people who are particularly sensitive to the diminishing daylight hours during the winter months. It is mainly among people living northern latitudes. This type of depression is intricately linked to the seasonal variations in natural light, and its impact on the circadian rhythm and neurotransmitter regulation.

People experiencing SAD often grapple with a range of symptoms, including pervasive feelings of sadness, lethargy, changes in sleep patterns, and a notable decrease in energy levels. The condition's prevalence underscores the significance of understanding its nuanced triggers and employing effective coping mechanisms.

It is important to realize that SAD is responsive to daily exposure to full spectrum lighting, which mimics natural sunlight. This therapeutic approach aims to mitigate the disruptions in circadian rhythms and melatonin production associated with the reduced daylight characteristic of winter. Light therapy has proven to be a valuable intervention, offering relief to many individuals affected by SAD and aiding in the regulation of mood-related neurotransmitters.

Moreover, recognizing the environmental and lifestyle factors that contribute to SAD is crucial. Implementing holistic strategies, such as outdoor activities, regular exercise, and dietary adjustments, can complement light therapy and contribute to a comprehensive approach in managing this condition. By delving into the intricate details of Seasonal Affective Disorder, we can better tailor interventions to address its multifaceted nature and enhance the well-being of those impacted by this seasonal challenge.

Tools To Lift Depression

Lifting depression can be accomplished through a combination of two approaches: 1) changing your perception of a situation; 2) the use of hypnosis to alter belief systems, clear emotional trauma, and develop inner resources. Learning to think in new ways as you develop a better relationship with yourself and with your world. You can develop a new way of being in the world. You can learn to be a functioning adult as well as healing the wounds of childhood. Developing high self-esteem as well as mastering the skills of adulthood are part of the process.

Because of the potential for suicide, it is particularly important for you to get professional help if you need it. When you are depressed, you generally have created a variety of issues in your life because of living with depression. The current issues need to be addressed as well as the older, more direct causes of the depression. Hypnosis is an excellent tool to search the subconscious for the origins of depression. Inner child work is very important in this process.

The foundation for acute depression is the denial of feelings, usually rooted in an early childhood event or environment. Years later, as adults, we unconsciously choose circumstances that recreate this early conflict, either in a similar pattern or in an attempt to avoid the similar pattern. In the latter case, we misinterpret why we are building our life in a particular way and end up in a trap. For example, a child raised in poverty may dedicate his/her life to acquiring riches to avoid fear and hopelessness. He/she may succeed in achieving wealth only to unconsciously experience that the journey was compulsive and without regard for important intrinsic values. Because depression develops with no apparent cause, it is often denied.

Repressed anger is often connected to depression. When tied to low self-esteem, the over-sensitivity of the depressed person creates even more reasons to feel anger which he/she continues to repress. The continuous buildup of anger in the form of depression further immobilizes a person or causes them to act out in another way (i.e. indifference or incompetence) so that they create circumstances that further damage self- esteem and generate more unexperienced anger. This passive-aggressive behavior is a pattern learned in childhood from rigid family and cultural values as a way of getting even for perceived inflicted hurts.

Learning to feel and express anger in a healthy way may relieve some of the tension but will not necessarily remove depression. Nor are all depressed people angry. In some cases, anger is overt. A depressed person may show outward hostility as a means of covering the underlying depression. Some patients exhibit resentment as a cloak for depression. Resentment differs from anger in that these people live with a distorted value system. They lack insight and are indifferent to the feelings of others. Control is often the theme, and they tend to focus on finding fault with others. The resentful person is more interested in getting even than discovering that he/she is de-pressed. Consequently, a depressed person who is resentful is very difficult to treat. In order to heal they must adapt a new set of values that include forgiveness and the removal of projection.

Because depression does not often provide a clear cause to the client, there is no place to direct the blame or reason for the depression. Particular to Western Europe and the United States, where our cultures teach individual responsibility, there is the tendency to manufacture feelings of guilt. It is very important to help the client to eliminate guilt. These feelings tend to make the clients feel "overly" responsible for their depression. This creates guilt.

In our society, guilt has been used to modify or control behavior. We are often brought up believe that feeling guilty is part of our conscious and keeps us on the straight and narrow. We think that somehow guilt makes us be better people. But really it is not guilt that keeps us from a life of crime, it is our values and ethics. Guilt has occupied a power position throughout most of our lives. If guilt improved our lives, we would not call the Dark Ages dark. That was a time when guilt ruled. In reality, guilt lowers your self-esteem and sets up you up for much greater depression. So, let's get rid of guilt. It really has no value. Shrink: GUILT down to a bad habit and eliminate it from your life!

Reframe Guilt as A Bad Habit

Steps in overcoming harmful habits

1. **Determine your current priority/direction.**
2. **Identify guilty feelings that are preventing you from moving forward**
3. **Which of these do you have a strong desire to let go of now?**

4. Focus on the guilt feelings that you are ready and willing to change.
5. Identify any satisfaction that you find in feeling guilty.
6. What must you remove to free yourself from guilty feelings?
7. What specific thoughts start guilty feelings?
8. Select a new way of thinking to eliminate guilty feelings.
9. What specific steps must you do to establish this new thinking pattern?
10. What elements would help to establish the new thinking pattern?

CHAPTER 4

ACHIEVE WEIGHT MASTERY

Understanding Weight

Weight is the number one problem facing Americans in a world that is plagued by starvation and malnutrition. Millions are spent each year as we try to solve this problem. We can send men to the Moon but up until now we can't achieve real weight mastery. People try diets, non-diets, exercise programs, etc. Yet the majority who let go of a significant amount of weight regain it and more within two years. Hypnosis to achieve weight mastery program is designed to solve the problem for life. The keys to do so lie in the subconscious mind. Most people think of themselves as their conscious mind. It seems to make their decisions and direct their activities, but the largest and most dominant part of the mind is the sub-conscious. The conscious mind only seems to call the shots, but people are ruled by the desires and the beliefs of subconscious. People make up rational reasons why they do things. Although the conscious mind could reason and decide on a course of action, it cannot put the decision into action unless the subconscious agrees and directs its energy towards the decision.

Our subconscious acts the way it is programmed to act, exactly as a computer, and most of this programming occurred before we were old enough to discriminate between ideas that were helpful and harmful to us. The subconscious accepts only what the conscious mind believes at the time - if the conscious mind changes, the subconscious mind will not change with it. If the two parts of the mind differ - the subconscious part will be the dominant one. It will continue to dictate our desires and behaviors. This is why the weight problem has not been solved before. It can only be solved by working with the subconscious.

Before we can start making the changes in the subconscious, we need to understand its nature and function. It was designed to be our servant, not our master. It consists of our desires, whims, emotions, and the energy that drives us. It has six vital functions, and we can use hypnosis, and meditation uses to achieve lasting weight mastery!

Functions of the Subconscious

- **<u>Serves as a Memory Bank-</u>** Here in the brain with the help of billions of tiny, interconnected nerve cells, everything that we have ever experienced is stored. The subconscious is the very cells of the body storing a maze of memory patterns which, when activated will feed information to the conscious mind. Nothing is ever erased unless the computer in the subconscious mind gives that command.

- **<u>Controls and Regulates the Involuntary Functions of the Body-</u>** breathing, circulation, metabolism, digestion, hormone balance, etc. Some of us who achieve weight mastery use these functions to speed up and improve these areas of the body.

- **<u>The Subconscious is the Seat of our Emotions-</u>** Since our emotions govern the strength of our desires, and these affect our behavior, many weight issues have a very strong emotional component and this is a key piece in solving the puzzle of and achieving weight mastery.

- **<u>It is the Home of the Imagination-</u>** Even when not used, each of us has a strong and active imagination that can be used in a positive way to create a compelling vision of the future self. Creative visualization is one of the greatest secrets of success. In the Achieve Weight Mastery Program we use this function to create and anchor the new body image in the subconscious for the conscious mind to duplicate.

- **<u>It Carries out Habitual Conduct-</u>** Using both direct & indirect suggestion in hypnosis we can create a system of habits that support and create Weight Mastery.
- **<u>The Subconscious is the Dynamo That Directs our Energy, the Energy Drives us Towards our Goals-</u>** It generates and releases energy, and it is not consciously directed, it is directed by circumstances and chance. Through positive reprogramming the subconscious is directed towards creating the goals to achieve weight mastery.

Kathy had lost the same 50 lbs. three times in her life. The weight would stay off for a few years and then slowly creep back on. She was sick of going up and down with her weight. Sick of having closets with different sized clothes. She wanted a permanent solution. She had discovered that she could lose weight, she just could not seem to keep it off. When we began working together, Kathy had a lot of negative self-talk and self judgement which we need to eliminate. Once that was completed, Kathy was able to quickly see the secret to keeping the weight off was in her sub conscious mind. We went through the functions of the subconscious and came up with plan for Kathy to master her weight so it would never be an issue again.

We used a clearing technique to remove all perceived failures from the memory banks and increase belief that she could be successful. That despite the yo yo dieting of the past, Kathy came to believe that this time she could be successful. This allowed us to get to her emotions and remove the deep emotional causes of eating. The powerful tool of imagination was used as Kathy imagined herself in her ideal body. She also placed a picture of herself at a lower weight on the refrigerator door. Kathy established healthy new habits by using self-talk and self-hypnosis. Five years later Kathy maintains her ideal healthy weight. When you master weight from the inside you do it for life!

Remember the Wheel of Personality? These parts of your personality are your inner voices. If you hear the voices in your head 99% of time it does not mean you are crazy.

It means you are self-aware. That is a very powerful place to be. Awareness gives you choice. We create our lives from the choices we make. Having the awareness about how your different parts feel about weight is very beneficial in giving you the tools to master your weight for your life. The following exercise will help you develop that awareness.

The Mandala Exercise

1. Determine and write the issue in the center of the table.
2. Listen to inner voices and write their messages.
3. Name the voices.
4. Write names of parts around the table.

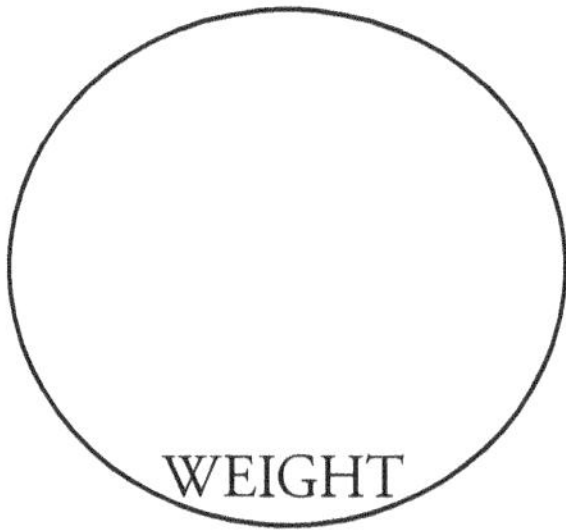

Part   **Statement about the issue:**

____

____

Weight is complex and the more you know about you the more successful you will be. Knowing your own crucial underlying issues is critical. Stepping completely out of judgement, get honest with yourself. These issues need to be resolve for lasting weight mastery. Look over this list carefully and determine what needs to be done.

Crucial Underlying Weight Issues

1. Lack of Primary Nurturing:

You are experiencing a longing for love. Food is perceived as a substitute for love. Your longing creates "hunger". Another possibility is you use food as a reward. This is usually accompanied by a lack of self-esteem and self-love.

Resolve through Inner Child, inner family bonding, and self-esteem work. It is critical that you learn to self-nurture and have true self love.

2. Stuffing Feelings:

You feel anxiety when anger, fear, guilt, pain, etc. are experienced and you do not know how to express the feelings. Food is used to "medicate" or "control" the feelings. Resolve stuffing feelings through clearing old feelings and learning to effectively express your feelings. It is important to educate yourself on appropriate ways to express feelings.

3. Protection:

You may fear being sexually attractive to the opposite sex. This may indicate childhood physical, sexual, or emotional abuse. You may also fear your own sexuality which can indicate conflicts among members of the "Committee". You may not trust people and want to keep them from getting close. Resolve by rewriting your inner stories. Talk to the parts of your personality to see how different parts of the Committee feel about weight. Work with your inner judge and rebel to end inner conflict.

4. Compulsive Eating as a part of Stress Patterns:

You may be experiencing generalized stress. Eating appears to be a reaction to stress. The Mindfulness exercise will help to end this pattern. You may be avoiding some productive activity such as creativity or emotional relationship. Resolve by learning to cope with stress factors. Create an internal safe place. Rewrite incidents to remove anxiety - develop inner resources. Talking with the parts can be very helpful. Ask yourself "Am I avoiding something else?"

Affirmations can be used to develop new habits.

5. Lifestyle Issues:

You come from a family with dysfunctional eating patterns and get little or no exercise. You eat fattening foods at inappropriate times in large quantities. Resolve by getting a realistic picture of appropriate eating and exercise. Educate yourself. Rewrite your inner stories that created the reactive patterns. Talking to your parts can be very helpful. Affirmations will help create new habits.

6. Self-Image Problems:

This is often based on negative criticism that you have received from others. You may think you have more of a weight problem when than you do. Your image of yourself may have been created by others. Resolve by discovering who gave you the idea you were overweight. Clear your programming from the past. Develop realistic self-concepts through education, self-hypnosis, and affirmations in your self-talk.

7. Metabolic Issues:

If you are more than fifty lbs. overweight, consult a doctor, natural health practitioner, or nutritionist. Obesity is now so common within the world's population that it is beginning to replace undernutrition and infectious diseases as the most significant contributor to ill health. Obesity is associated with diabetes mellitus, coronary heart disease, certain forms of cancer, and sleep-breathing disorders. Obesity is defined by a body-mass index (weight divided by square of the height) of 30 $kg\ m^{-2}$ or greater, but this does not consider the morbidity and mortality associated with more modest degrees of overweight, nor the detrimental effect of intra-abdominal fat. The global epidemic of obesity results from a combination of genetic susceptibility, increased availability of high-energy foods, high sugar, and decreased requirement for physical activity in modern society. Obesity should no longer be regarded simply as a cosmetic problem affecting certain individuals, but an epidemic that threatens global well-being. Some people are wired for obesity. If this seems to be you, I encourage you to do further research. You can resolve some of these issues by self-hypnosis, self-talk affirmations, and advanced neuroscience techniques to speed up your metabolism. You can also use direct self-suggestion to increase exercise, change beliefs and work with the body to speed up metabolism. It is important to look at your lifestyle and develop changes that will work for you. Change is a constant process in our environment and our lives. Yet, in the midst of all this change, some of us cling to old habits and beliefs no matter how much pain they cause.

For Bob it was all about compulsive eating as the main way he coped with stress. His doctor recommended that he lose 35 to 40 lbs., reduce his stress levels and start to exercise regularly. As hard as he tried, he could not make any progress. His work was very stressful, he traveled a lot, and ate out a lot. When he came to me he was very discouraged. I was glad to be able to share that I, myself, had lost 150 lbs. and kept it off.

We focused on Bob learning to manage his stress and changing some lifestyle choices.

I taught him breathing techniques and made customized stress reduction MP3 which he used regularly. Bob began daily meditation, starting with 5 minutes and working up to 20 minutes. He also began to walk 20 minutes a day five times a week. Bob also made some changes with his friendships. He realized that he had outgrown some people and was able to make some new friends with similar goals of wanting a more physically active lifestyle. In eight months, Bob lost that 40 lbs. and significantly improved his life by using his mind.

For Amanda it was really the first three underlying issues. She lacked a sense being loved and nurtured. She had learned to used food to feed her inner hunger. She also stuffed her negative feelings, often letting others take advantage of her. Her weight was also protection against being hurt. Although Amanda longed for love she feared rejection so much she kept people away from her. Her self-esteem was very poor. She constantly focused on her weight and made it what created her value. We began with a self-esteem intensive program. I will talk more the program in the next chapter.

For now, the most important point is that your self-esteem is the foundation of what you can create in your life. You can only get in life what you really think you deserve. Amanda worked with me as a success coaching client for a year. She lost the weight, developed super self-esteem, and changed her lifestyle to include new friends, exercise, meditation, and journaling.

Effectiveness of Hypnosis in Weight Mastery*

This study examined the effect of adding hypnosis to a behavioral weight-management program on short- and long-term weight change.

One hundred nine subjects, who ranged in age from 17 to 67, completed a behavioral treatment either with or without the addition of hypnosis. At the end of the 9-week program, both interventions resulted in significant weight reduction. However, at the 8-month and 2-year follow-ups, the hypnosis clients showed significant additional weight loss, while those in the behavioral treatment exhibited little further change. More of the subjects who used hypnosis also achieved and maintained their personal weight goals. The utility of employing hypnosis as an adjunct to a behavioral weight-management program is discussed.

* From The New England Journal of Medicine

Learning Self-Hypnosis for Weight Mastery:

Hypnosis is the most practical and the most effective way to subconscious change. Since the subconscious has no power to discriminate it will believe anything that it is told in the correct manner. A key piece in working with the subconscious is the self-hypnosis that you practice. The tools that you use are suggestion, concentration, and imagination. The fastest, easiest, and most successful way for you to learn self-hypnosis is through creating a post hypnotic suggestion. This a suggestion combined with images you give to yourself in a meditative state.

Guidelines for Structuring Self-Hypnosis Suggestions:

- Motivating desire must be strong. Before you use a suggestion think about why you want it to happen.
- Always be positive/enthusiastic.
- Always use the present or progressive present tense. Imagine yourself achieving the goal now.
- Suggest action. See yourself in the act of doing what you want.
- Be specific.
- Keep language simple and direct.
- Fuel visualizations and suggestions with positive emotions.
- Use repetition especially of words and phrases important to you!

Suggestions to Learn Until They Become Habits:

- I awaken immediately in case of any emergency, alert, and normal in every way.
- I go into hypnosis quickly and easily every time I practice it.
- I awaken in exactly (time) minutes awake, refreshed, and fully conscious.

Keys to Effective Suggestions:

1. **Use only positive, present tense words.** (Present progressive is okay.) Instead of suggesting what is NOT wanted, suggest the positive outcome.
2. **Use simple, exciting words.** Suggestions are more powerful when they are delivered in an excited, confidant tone.
3. **Avoid words like "try" and "should."** Use words like *"easy," "fun,"* and *"effortless"* instead.
4. **Include as many of your senses as possible (multisensory).** The more multisensory you can make it, the more real it will be.
5. **Use repetitive word or phrases.** Three-word phrases are particularly effective *("clear, clean, fresh").* Be repetitive. Be repetitive. Be repetitive.
6. **Include a direct image of the desired state.** Suggest a precise picture of you are experiencing the desired goal. (e.g., *"See yourself right now....."*

Achieve Weight Mastery Self Hypnosis Exercise

    A. **Close your eyes**
    B. **Take in three deep breathes**
    C. **Count backwards from 10 to 1**
    D. **Relax your body**
    E. **Clear your mind**
    F. **Say your suggestion and imagine your visualizations.**
    G. **Count yourself back from 1 to 5**

Suggestion: (1 powerful affirmation) **Visualizations:** (3 images)

Sample Action Plan

- Listen to the Achieve Weight Mastery MP3 5 x a week (link at bottom)
- Use a food diary for first thirty days. No judgement just awareness
- Drink plenty of water each day.
- Take small bites and chew slowly (twenty times plus)
- Exercise twenty continuous minutes (fast walking is excellent)
- Newest studies say you will get results if you do this at least 2 x a week
- Lower fat intake to 10% to 20% total fat calories.
- Eat healthy meals – find your eating pattern after emotional and stress eating are removed. Enjoy protein low calorie snacks mid-morning and mid-afternoon.
- Eat most of your calories earlier in the day.
- Weigh yourself once a week

Copy this link into your browser and download free MP3 http://zoilitagrant.net/media/files/10Achieve Weight Mastery/dlcd10.htm

Exercises that really work.

1. What Is Hunger?

Relax and focus your attention on your teeth. Then focus your attention on your mouth. Are there any sensations in that area that you would call hunger? Any messages that say it is time to eat—or just comfortable and full? Can you tell the difference? Are you thirsty? Now focus your attention on your throat. Are there any sensations that you would call hunger? Time to eat? Comfortable? Full? Now focus your attention on your stomach. What sensations do you experience in this area? What do you associate with these sensations? Now move your attention to your abdomen. Put your hands on your abdomen and rub it a bit. What sensations do you experience there? What do you associate these sensations with? Are you hungry? Are you thirsty? Are you comfortable? Are you full? Now rub both hands on the entire area. On a scale of zero to ten, with zero being empty, five comfortable, and ten being stuffed—at what level of hunger is your body right now? On a scale of zero to ten, with zero being pleasant, five okay and ten being terrific—how do you feel right now? Is there a relationship between your level of hunger and your state of being?

2. The Hunger Scale Discovering your own hunger level

Check in with your body before you eat: listen to your body's response. Eat only when hungry—at zero. Often you may find that you are thirsty, not hungry. When in doubt, DON'T EAT. Eat when you feel zero to five and you will lose weight. If you have trouble hitting zero, don't eat for an evening, allowing yourself to experience hunger.

0   5   10

Empty   Comfortable   Stuffed

3. Self-Image Exercises

- **<u>Stop Look & Listen-</u>** Whenever you have negative thoughts about your body, picture a red stop sign, look at all of your good characteristics in your mind, listen to the sound of your own voice supporting you and validating you.
- **<u>Celebrate a Feature-</u>** Each week pick something about yourself, your personality or the things you can do and celebrate it. Honor that characteristic for the week and remind yourself of its value.
- **Self-Empowerment Exercise**
1. Enter self-hypnosis through deep physical relaxation.
2. Visualize a large room in their mind to store their thoughts.
3. Deepen into subconscious.
4. Visualize a beautiful white beach. A great golden sun with only healthy rays are shining down upon you
5. Deepen to connect the surf, sun, sea birds, etc.....
6. Bring attention to the left foot and radiate golden sunlight up the body to the brain and down the right side of the body to the right foot.
7. Use self-esteem affirmations

8. Go meet your future self with super self-esteem.
9. Return to normal consciousness

4. Breathing Exercises Quieting Breath:

Deep Rhythmic Breathing - matching inhalation and exhalation

Alternate nostril breathing

Close off one side of your nose and breathe in through the other. Then switch sides.

Breathing Exercise to Eliminate Impulsiveness:

Inhale 1...2...3...4...
Hold 1...2...3...4...
Exhale 1...2...3...4...5...6...7...8...
Hold 1...2...3...4...
Inhale 1...2...3...4...
Hold 1...2...3...4...
Exhale 1...2...3...4...5...6...7...8...
Hold 1...2...3...4...

Repeat cycles for 5 to 10 minutes Start with 1 minute build to 10 minutes

5. Walking Exercise

- **<u>The Easy Way</u>**

No sweat, no pain you simply commit to a 45 min. comfortable walk five to seven times a week. Develop a walk with a friend or learn to contemplate your life while you balance your body. Start with five or ten minutes and work your way up to 45. Keep your pace moderate so you feel like doing the distance.

- **<u>Get Fit Quick</u>**

Take several short walks throughout the day. Do either three ten min walks or two fifteen min walks five to seven days a week, since your metabolism speeds up after you stop. This is both super for energy and balancing your weight. Walk twenty to thirty minutes, varying your pace- walk briskly for one min, comfortably for three mins, and build from there in this ratio. Walk five to seven days a week. This will work up a sweat and is doubly effective when combined with visualization.

In a faraway Native American village, a woman found herself torn between opposing desires that pulled her in different directions. One part of her longed for the thrill of learning and personal growth, while the other sought the safety of familiarity and a reluctance to change. Uncertain about which path to take, she turned to the village's wise woman, hoping to find guidance in navigating her inner conflict.

Pouring out her heart, the woman shared her internal struggle with the wise woman. With a timeless wisdom that transcended generations, the wise woman revealed a profound truth about the human experience. She spoke of the dual nature within each person—an interplay between a dark wolf and a light wolf. These internal forces continually vied for attention, influencing the choices that would ultimately shape the course of one's life.

The wise woman stressed that the outcome of this inner conflict rested on the choices individuals make. Life unfolds through these decisions, and the wolf that emerges triumphant is the one we consciously choose to nurture and feed. Armed with this profound insight, the native woman gained a newfound clarity, ready to make choices that would carve out her destiny. Remember the wolf we feed is always the one that wins!

CHAPTER 5

THEORIES OF ADDICTION

An addiction is a repetitive behavior over which you have very little control, and which is in some way destructive to you. There are several theories about what causes addictions to develop. All these theories are partly true, and we need to address each of these when we need to pursue lasting recovery. Since our goal is both to create a healthy life and maintain it, we need to address the following:

- **Habit**

Originally, addictions were looked upon as bad habits. Under this theory, the only difference between a nail biter and an alcoholic was merely one of degree. Addicts were seen as being morally weak and having little willpower. Ranging from clients with smoking and weight issues to those with alcohol and drug challenges, all were seen as needing to develop the "willpower" necessary to end these problems. To address the habit aspects of the addicted part of the personality, we use direct suggestion work and mental reprogramming. This is very effective in helping clients to develop the self-control and self-management skills necessary to affect this cause of the addiction.

- **Disease**

Much of our information on the disease model of addiction comes from the research and work done with alcoholics. According to this theory, an addiction is seen as genetic and possibly hereditary. Substances or behavior are regarded as toxic. There is much scientific research to support this theory. Research shows that addicts seem to lack enzymes to properly metabolize certain substances—alcohol, foods or nicotine—which cause toxic reactions resulting in craving. We also know that the livers of some people process substances differently causing a biochemical reaction that resembles an allergy. Under this theory, it is necessary for the individual to abstain from the substance forever. There is no moral weakness implied. In a way, the "addiction" is viewed as not really the client's fault. This area needs to be addressed by helping your client to change the life-style patterns to maintain sobriety. In some cases, your clients will need to be involved in programs that promote abstinence. The most effective treatment for abstinence is involvement in a support group such as any of the 12 Step-Programs.

- **Unmet Emotional Needs**

David Quigley, founder of Alchemical Hypnotherapy, was one of the first put forth the theory that an addiction was an attempt to deal with unmet emotional needs—most likely resulting from the trauma of childhood or other wounding experiences. Under this theory, you are either attempting to meet basic needs, or to numb the pain of unmet needs through addictive behavior. Using this theory, the most effective tool is to do Subpersonality Work and to use the Parts Work exercise presented in this book.

- **Spiritual Wound**

The last theory of addiction comes from John Bradshaw. In his book "Homecoming," he says that there is a spiritual wound in the person resulting in addictive behavior. This wound causes a disconnection from the Inner Self. People then try to develop a sense of self through relationships with substances, activities, people or things. This theory takes into consideration the broad spectrum of codependency and addictive behavior which allows us to extend our work into a much broader base of client issues. The most effective treatment to heal the spiritual wound involves connecting to your Inner Self and to address the aspects of habits, genetic propensity, and unmet emotional needs. Working with your issues around addiction requires great flexibility. Effective work needs to be tailor-made for you.

Identify the problems:	**Work to eliminate habits:**
What is its cause?	Support the recovery of emotional wound
What is its effect?	Find a Spiritual connection
What is the solution?	Help the body to balance

The Source Guidance / Intuition

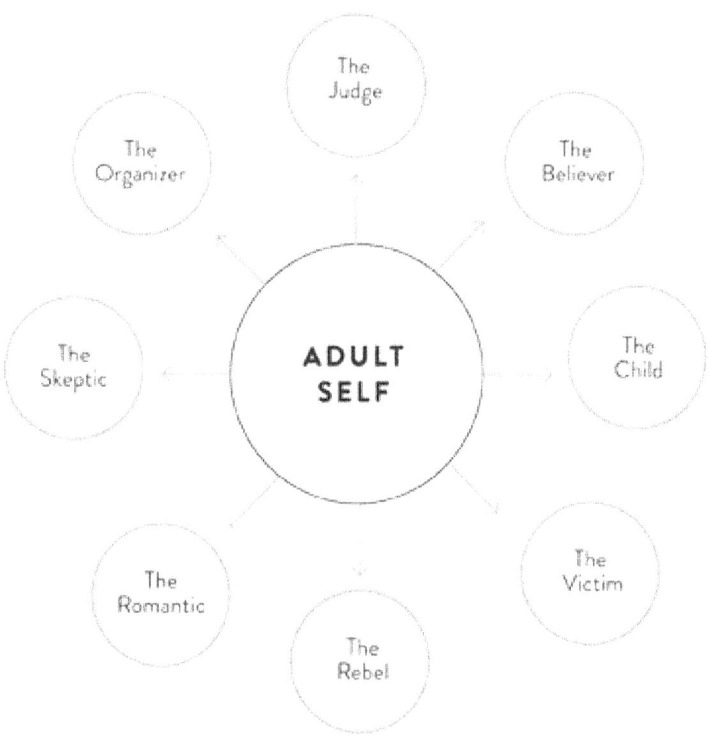

Address **Habits** by building a strong adult self who can change behaviors.

Address **Disease** by abstinence when necessary and changing lifestyle.

Address **Unmet Emotional Needs** through Subpersonality Work, Emotional Clearing and Cellular Block Clearing Technique.

Address the **Spiritual Wound** through reconnecting to the Source/Guidance and developing Inner Resources, Guides, Angels, Higher Self, 12 Step Programs

Accurate assessment is critical for lasting recovery. The more you can stay out of self-judgement the more you can clearly see.

<u>Habits:</u> The habits show up through the actions of the parts.

There are two different parts that can be involved in the addictive behavior patterns. Each of these is different and requires an individual strategy to work with it.

A. Addicted/Wounded Parts

The addicted or wounded parts are often the aspects of us that finds pleasure in certain behaviors. The behaviors are used to address emotional needs or heal spiritual wounds. These behaviors are known as coping mechanisms, and they are widespread among individuals grappling with addiction. It's important to recognize that this is a prevalent aspect in many cases of addiction.

Let's delve deeper into the concept of addicted or wounded parts. These aspects of us often gravitate towards certain behaviors not just for momentary pleasure, but to cope with unmet emotional needs or to mend spiritual wounds. In essence, these behaviors serve as coping mechanisms, offering a temporary relief or distraction from underlying issues.

Imagine these addicted or wounded parts as fragments of your personality seeking solace or fulfillment through specific actions. Whether it's turning to substances, people, activities, or habits, these behaviors become a refuge, attempting to address the void left by emotional struggles or spiritual emptiness. It's crucial to understand that this inclination towards coping mechanisms is a widespread phenomenon in the realm of addiction. Many of us find ourselves tangled in these patterns, often unaware that our behaviors are intricately linked to deeper emotional or spiritual struggles. By acknowledging and exploring these aspects, you can embark on a journey of self-discovery and healing, unraveling the layers of complexity that contribute to addictive behaviors.

Jean was a compulsive overeater. She had done tons of therapy, self-help, diet and programs galore. So far, the best help she had found, was Overeaters Anonymous.

She attended meetings regularly and it was helping her to stabilize her eating patterns, so she quit gaining. Jean wanted more. She told me she wanted to "shed the blanket of fat" she had been carrying for years. Since Jean was very open to hypnosis, we began immediately to look for the root causes of her addictive eating patterns.

Being the youngest of seven children, Jean was practically raised by her older brothers and sisters. She was five years younger than her next sister, so no one really wanted play with her, and all considered her a bother. They often handed her food when she wanted attention. This probably established the pattern of her turning to food for comfort. As an overweight child in a family of overweigh people, food was the main focus of her life. Food was a way to nurture and comfort herself. Since she was healing her Spiritual Wound through her work with Overeaters Anonymous, we focused our work on healing Jean's subconscious unmet emotional needs.

Through intensive self-esteem work, using a self-talk menu and self-hypnosis Jean was able to completely change her relationship with food. She used a free tracking device on her phone to track her food. This always needs to be done without judgement. The amount of self-awareness it gives you, is the tool that helps you make conscious choices. Once she healed emotional eating and eliminated anxiety, she could easily make conscious eating choices. If Jean can do this, why not you?

Shadow Parts/Saboteurs

This is that part of you that acts in ways to harm, punish, or even destroy you. It is a matter of degree from letting a food binge sidetrack your weight mastery goals to driving while drinking. They both involve your self-destructive side. Your shadow does not necessary enjoys the addictive behaviors, he/she wants to hurt you. The sole purpose of the self-destructive shadow is to hurt you. It is a saboteur. This part of you may appear to be either powerless or very controlling. It can show up as either a victim or an egomaniac.

When dealing with our own shadow, it is necessary to build a deep connection with our shadow and then change self-hatred into self-love. That is why building self-esteem is so important in recovery. Understand why you have inner anger, by looking at what you did or didn't do. This involves deep self-discovery, identifying unresolved incidences in the past without judgement. Your saboteur is attempting to punish you for things that happened in the past. Revisit the incidents, learn from them, resolve them, and let go.

The saboteur intensifies when important needs are not being met and when needs are being repressed. As you develop more self-awareness and strengthen your adult self you can meet with your "Committee" the members of the Wheel of Personality. The saboteur can then express needs and negotiate lifestyle changes. Even if it feels uncomfortable it is important to work with your shadows and saboteurs. They become more dangerous when repressed or ignored.

Andy knew he had a saboteur. His shadow was running his life into the ground.

He was smart and talented, but was constantly late on projects and unprepared for important meetings. He had extreme anxiety and took several medications. Andy was constantly telling everyone that he was his own worst enemy. Lucky for Andy, his company realized his potential. They were willing to help Andy realize that potential. They authorized 10 sessions of coaching with me. We discovered that Andy was filled with self-hatred built upon messages that he got from his abusive and angry father. As Andy began to change his negative self-talk to positive affirmations, his job performance improved. Andy became his own best friend. After the first 10 sessions were up, Andy continued with another 10 that he scheduled and paid for himself. The results were truly remarkable. Andy renovated his life through changes in his thought processes and making different lifestyle choices.

Disease: This is the biochemical element, the physical addictions.

Biochemical addiction happens when our bodies become reliant on a substance, like sugar, in a way that affects how our brains work. It's like the body gets used to having that substance and starts to crave it, even if it's not good for us. This shows up in food and drink. Understanding how our bodies can get addicted to sugar is crucial because sugar is everywhere, and many of us eat more of it than we realize. Too much sugar can lead to health problems like obesity and diabetes. By learning about biochemical addiction to sugar, we can make better choices about what we eat and take care of our bodies. Recent research from places like the Mayo Clinic indicate Blood Sugar levels contribute to heart attacks and Heart Disease.

Sugar addiction is when a person craves and depends on sugar in a way that it starts affecting their daily life and health. Many people don't realize how common it is. It's not just about liking sweets; it's about the body wanting more and more sugar, even when it's not good for us.

Our bodies process sugar in a way that involves complex biochemical reactions. When we eat sugary foods, our bodies break down the sugar into smaller parts, and this process affects how our brains work. Neurotransmitters, which are like messengers in our brains, play a big role in this. They help send signals that tell our bodies how to react to the sugar we've eaten. Dopamine is a special neurotransmitter that plays a key role in the brain's reward system. When we eat sugary foods, our brains release dopamine, making us feel good. This good feeling is a reward for eating something sweet. Over time, our brains start connecting this pleasure with sugar, and that's when the cycle of craving and addiction can begin. Understanding this connection helps us see why we might crave sugar even when we don't need it and why it can be hard to resist those sweet treats. To change the pattern, we need to work with the subconscious.

When it comes to satisfying your sweet tooth, consider opting for healthier alternatives. Instead of reaching for sugary snacks, try sweetening your food with natural options like raw honey or maple syrup (not good for alcoholics or diabetics). There are other natural products like monk fruit which are available in health food stores. You can also snack on fruits like apples, berries, or dried fruits as a tasty and nutritious substitute for candies or cookies.

Addressing sugar addiction requires the support of those around us. Families and schools play a crucial role in helping individuals make healthier choices. Families can encourage balanced eating habits at home, while schools can educate students about the impact of excessive sugar consumption. Together, these support systems create an environment that fosters positive habits and well-being.

<u>Unmet Emotional Needs:</u>

This involves deepening your awareness and seeing your own subconscious motivations. An excellent way of doing this become aware of and learn to work with your parts…..your Committee!

Understanding Parts

Each human being is made up of different parts. These different parts, or sub personalities, work together like a committee inside of the person. Each part or sub personality has their own agenda, and, in many people, there is only a thin thread of memory connecting the parts. Ordinary people shift from one sub personality to another without clear awareness. Since each part is characterized by its own beliefs, attitudes, and feelings, it develops an independent identity. There is a tendency to think that when you are being a certain part that this is who you are. The Rebel experiences the world through his/her filters and forgets that there are other parts of you. The Rebel wants the Rebel's agenda to rule the client's life, even if it is not in the best interest of the whole self.

People get lost in their parts. Each part has distinct functions, beliefs and feelings that are based on early life experiences. They can become polarized and contaminated, creating struggle within the personality for control. The less integrated a human being is, the more rigid and unconscious the parts are. For example, the contaminated Rebel only wants the Rebel's way. People have many different parts depending upon childhood experiences, external circumstances, programming, and spiritual development. There are some standard parts that most people possess. These are divided into intellectual and feeling parts. Intellectual parts are analytical, they focus on goals and believe that the emotions aren't important. Feeling parts experience the world through their bodies and are constantly trying to achieve pleasure and avoid pain.

Common Parts

Intellectual	Feeling
The Judge	The Child
The Believer	The Rebel
The Skeptic	The Victim
The Organizer	The Romantic

Meeting the Committee Exercise

1. Enter a relaxed state and go to a committee room where the parts can meet.
2. Observe the parts. (Judge, etc.)
3. Have the client (as adult self) speak with the parts about a goal.
4. Have the adult take charge of the committee
5. Deepen for your suggestions and visualizations.
6. Return to normal consciousness.

Connecting with your parts and managing them is the secret to healing deep wounds.

<u>Spiritual Wound:</u>

Understanding your Spiritual Wound and how to heal it.

In life, we often encounter challenges that go beyond the physical and emotional aspects, reaching into the realm of the spiritual. A spiritual wound is a deep hurt that affects our innermost selves, impacting our sense of purpose, connection, and inner peace. It might stem from experiences like loss, betrayal, or a profound sense of disconnection. Spiritual wounds disconnect us from our sense of the Source, the Divine. The spiritual wound is like an invisible injury, affecting our core beliefs and values. It can leave us feeling lost, questioning our purpose, and struggling to find meaning in life. Identifying this type of wound is crucial for initiating the healing process.

Take time to reflect on the source of the spiritual wound. Journaling or deep introspection can help you understand the roots of the pain. Recognizing and acknowledging the wound is the first step towards healing. Reach out to friends, family, or mentors who can provide emotional support. Discussing your feelings with someone you trust can offer different perspectives and alleviate the burden of the spiritual wound.

Spending time in nature can be a powerful way to heal spiritually. Whether it's a walk in the park, sitting by a river, or simply enjoying the beauty of the outdoors, nature has a way of soothing the soul and promoting inner peace. Twenty minutes walking in nature is an excellent way to clear your mind while you soothe your Soul.

Meditation is an excellent tool. Engage in mindfulness practices to center yourself and cultivate a sense of inner calm. These practices can help you detach from the turmoil of the spiritual wound and find a peaceful space within. Focusing on the positive aspects of life and practicing gratitude can shift your perspective. Despite the pain, acknowledging the things you are grateful for can bring a sense of balance and healing.

For some, reconnecting with faith or exploring spirituality can be a source of comfort and healing. This might involve attending religious services, reading spiritual texts, or participating in activities that align with your beliefs.

Creative outlets, such as art, music, or writing, can provide a means of expressing and processing the emotions tied to the spiritual wound. Engaging in artistic expression can be a cathartic and healing experience.

Remember, healing from a spiritual wound is a gradual process that requires patience and self-compassion. By combining self-reflection, support from others, and various healing strategies, you can embark on a journey towards spiritual well-being and a renewed sense of purpose.

As we grow up, the journey toward becoming a fully functioning adult becomes a significant and crucial part of our lives. It's not just about reaching a certain age; it's about developing the skills, mindset, and responsibilities needed to navigate the challenges of the world. Here are a few reasons why this transition is so important: becoming a fully functioning adult allows us to be independent. Independence means being able to make our own choices, take care of ourselves, and handle life's responsibilities. It's about becoming the captain of our own ship.

With adulthood comes greater responsibility. We start to take charge of our lives, managing tasks like work, finances, and personal relationships. Being responsible means understanding the impact of our actions and making choices that contribute positively to our lives and the lives of those around us. The journey to adulthood is a journey of personal growth. It's about discovering who we are, what we value, and what we want from life. This growth comes from experiences, challenges, and learning how to overcome obstacles.

Fully functioning adults play a crucial role in society. They contribute through their work, relationships, and civic engagement. Whether it's in the workplace, community, or family, adults can make a positive impact. As adults, we form deeper and more meaningful relationships. This includes friendships, romantic partnerships, and familial bonds. Being a fully functioning adult means navigating these relationships with maturity, empathy, and effective communication.

The journey to becoming a fully functioning adult is not a destination but a continuous process of learning and adapting. As adults we can engage in lifelong learning, staying curious, and seeking new knowledge and skills throughout their lives. Self-reliance is a key aspect of adulthood. It means being confident in our abilities to solve problems, make decisions, and face challenges.

This self-reliance is empowering and contributes to a sense of fulfillment and accomplishment. A fully functioning adult is more likely to experience overall well-being and happiness. This stems from a combination of factors, including a sense of purpose, positive relationships, and the ability to navigate life's ups and downs with resilience. In essence, becoming a fully functioning adult is a journey that shapes the course of our lives. It's about embracing independence, taking on responsibilities, and contributing to the world in a meaningful way. By doing so, we not only enhance our own lives but also contribute to the well-being of the broader community.

A fully functioning adult can be defined as an individual who has three core beliefs and four skill sets. These are called the **Significant Seven***

Beliefs:

1. **1. I believe that I am worthwhile, valuable and I am significant in my relationships.**
2. **I believe that I am capable and competent.**
3. **I believe that I can influence the course of my own life.**

Skills:

1. **Strong intra-personal skills**. The ability to understand personal emotions, to use that understanding to develop self-discipline and self-control, and to delay gratification.
2. **Strong interpersonal skills**. The ability to work with others and develop friendships through communication, cooperation, negotiation, sharing, empathizing and listening. Couple ship skills are included.

3. **Strong systemic skills.** The ability to respond to the limits and consequences of everyday life with responsibility, adaptability, flexibility and integrity.

4. **Strong wisdom skills.** The ability to use wisdom and to evaluate situations according to appropriate values to learn from the experiences of life. The ability to make decisions and choices based on values and goals not moods and circumstances.

*** Based upon ideas in Developing Capable Young People by Stephen Glenn**

<u>**The Recovery Steps**</u>

- **Stop all destructive behavior.**
- **End all denial.**
- **Do the feeling work.**
- **Re-parent yourself.**
- **Decontaminate the parts of the self.**
- **Develop fully functioning relationships.**
- **Have a spiritual awakening.**

Recovery Self-Assessment

Name: _________________________   Phone: ___________________

1. My Story.

____

____

____

____

____

____

2. What is the nature and extent of the issue in your life? Has it ever changed?

____

____

____

____

____

____

3. Under what circumstances does the issue tend to be more intense? (When? Where? With whom? Why? How?)

____

____

____

____

____

____

4. Do people you know have similar issues? (Friends, co-workers, significant others, parents, children, etc.) Do you know anyone personally who had their life negatively affected by an issue like this? Do you know anyone who has mastered an issue like this?

____

____

____

____

____

____

5. Who in your life supports you in your recovery? How do you experience their support? What kind of support is best for you?

____

____

____

____

____

____

6. What other kinds of recovery methods have you tried? What has been the effect? How do you feel about them.

____

____

____

____

____

____

7. What lifestyle or attitude changes have been partially successful? Are you willing to make life-style changes?

____

____

____

____

____

____

8. How much exercise do you get each week? How's your diet? How are your sleeping patterns?

____

____

____

____

____

9. When was your last physical examination/health care consultation? Are you under the care of a health care professional? Are you on any medication?

____

____

____

____

____

____

10. How do you feel about your family of origin?

____

____

____

____

____

____

11. Have you ever felt physically, mentally, sexually, or emotionally abused? Write about your experience.

____

____

____

____

____

____

12. What are your Spiritual, Philosophical or Religious beliefs like?

____

____

____

____

____

____

13. Do you associate any of these emotions with your issue? (circle)

Boredom	Glamour	Embarrassment	Fear
Frustration	Depression	Loneliness	Happiness
Loss, Grief	Femininity	Masculinity	Abandonment
Romance	Relaxation	Sadness	Anger
Shame	Anxiety	Guilt	

Other Emotions:

14. Is there anything else you would like to say?

____

____

____

____

____

____

15. What are your goals?

____

____

____

____

____

____

Remember the importance of:

Recovery Steps
Recovery Tools
Life-style choices

The Recovery Tool:

Mindfulness Exercise

Sit in a comfortable relaxed position. You can sit either on the floor with your legs crossed or in a chair. Rest your hands lightly on your thighs with the palms down. Cast your eyes down but leave them slightly open. Focus your attention on your breath. Breathe deeply rhythmically. Quiet your mind by focusing on your breath. As thoughts appear, bring your attention gently back to your breath. After your period of open-eyed mindfulness, close your eyes and visualize your weight goal. Use this time to reinforce goal with positive affirmations. Practice for at least 10 minutes 2 X a day. Work up to 20 minutes. 2 X a day.

Benefits:

Improves ability to handle stress.
Gives emotional space. Allows you to handle emotions better.
Cuts down on reactivity and triggering.
Improves concentration and focus.
Supports immune system functioning and body's ability to handle disease.

Recovery Yoga

1. Grounding Pose
2. Salute
3. Earth Touching
4. Horse Pose
5. Warrior Two on each side
6. Salute
7. Triangle Pose on each side
8. Salute
9. Grounding Pose

Be Yourself.
Accept Yourself.
Value Yourself.
Forgive Yourself.
Bless Yourself.
Express Yourself.
Trust Yourself.
Love Yourself.
Empower Yourself.

Lifestyle Choices:

Self-Esteem and Empowerment

Webster defines empowerment as "to give power, to enable." Power is the ability to do or act with vigor, influence, and strength. A self-empowered person is one who has fully integrated the role of the "Adult

Self" into his or her life. Self-empowered people see themselves as the cause of the results of their lives. They are responsible for what happens to them. When things don't go as planned, they remain reasonable in their choices in dealing with all the circumstances of their lives. It is this *belief* that they *do* have choices that opens the door to self-empowerment.

This attitude of personal responsibility and freedom of choice leads self-empowered people to fulfillment and joy in their lives. They may experience unexpected tragedies, but probably less than most. Even under the most difficult of circumstances, their belief in their ability to choose the best actions and their positive attitude, guides them through life's challenges. Self-empowered people have a vision of what they want from life. They create goals to measure their progress and develop strategies that help them achieve these goals. Each of us has the innate ability to do the same.

The dark side of empowerment is living life as a victim. Victims believe that they cannot do anything about their lives. Something outside of them controls their feelings, thoughts, actions, and circumstances. Viewing life as a victim can be painful, often perpetuating anger, desperation, depression, and hopelessness.

Self-empowered people move toward what they want, toward pleasure, and *generate* more positive energy as part of the process. Victims believe they have limited choices. They move away from pain, discomfort, and fear. Acting out of avoidance *depletes* their energy. If these are the differences between a self-empowered person and a victim, then what are the causes for these differences?

One of the fundamental underlying causes is that victims are often disconnected from their Inner Selves, and they operate with negative belief systems. To become truly self-empowered, they must make a connection with their spirits and change negative, often unconscious beliefs about themselves and the world. As they build empowerment, they build self-esteem.

Self-esteem can be divided into three different components.

1. **Self-Image** is the picture that we have of ourselves in our minds. In women, this is about 70% body image, but also includes

characteristics that we identify with ourselves such as hard-working or lazy. In men, it is approximately 50% body image and 50%-character traits.

2. **Self-confidence** is measured by the things we know we can do. The world reinforces us by giving us money, grades or pats on the back.

3. The third component is **Innate Worth**. This is an intrinsic sense of worth and value that comes from within our self and is not dependent on externals.

Affirmations Which Support the Development of High Self Esteem:

1. *I believe that I am capable and competent.*
2. *I believe that I am worthwhile and valuable, and that my life is significant.*
3. *I believe that I have the power to influence my life.*

Do 3 sets of 10 each every day. Just like physical muscles, you build emotional muscles in sets.

Nine Things You Can Do to Increase Your Self-Esteem

1. Increase the number of positive things you say to yourself about yourself.
2. Decrease the number of negative things you say to yourself about your weaknesses.
3. Practice giving and receiving genuine compliments.
4. Develop a more realistic view of the world and your place in it.
   - Develop an appreciation of your own worth.
   - Accept that you are not responsible for the emotional reaction of others.
5. Accept your weaknesses and mistakes.
6. Learn to refrain from comparing yourself to others.
7. Work at reducing indecisiveness.
8. Limit the number of commitments you make.
9. Use your imagination—spend time regularly recalling your successes.

Tips to Improve Self-Esteem

- **Focus On your Positives!**

  It's easy to forget that you are a special person. Take some time to write a list of the attributes that you are proud of (i.e., intelligence, humor, athletic ability, etc.) Be specific and keep your list handy to make additions or read it aloud when you are feeling down.

- **Look In the Mirror!**

  Take a reflective moment to see you as others do. Are you taking care of your body; are you eating right, exercising, and practicing good grooming? How you look on the outside is a reflection on how you feel about yourself on the inside.

- **Associate with Winners!**

  Picking positive friends and associates helps to surround yourself with positive energy, enthusiasm and a "can do" attitude. Be careful not to compare, be okay with who you are.

- **Manage Your First Impressions!**

  Many studies in human communications emphasize the importance of a first impression. Look people in the eye, reach out with a handshake and volunteer your name first. Try to use the person's name in the conversation to aid in remembering. Using this technique gives a great first impression. Eye contact is vital in informing people how you feel about yourself and conveys sincerity.

- **Acknowledge Those Around You!**

  Take the time to notice the little positives you see in others. Don't be stingy with compliments and congratulations. By putting the positive energy out to others, you are bound to receive some back. Say "Thank You" when you are the receiver of praise.

- **Choose Your Words Wisely!**

Everything you say about yourself, and others is carved into your memory. Negative self-talk, along with put downs of other people has a way of influencing the way you look at life.

Self Esteem Development Sheet

1. List three things you like about yourself. (New things each week.)

____

____

____

____

____

____

2. List three successes you have achieved this week. (New successes each week)

____

____

____

____

____

____

3. List one good habit you are working on.

____

____

____

____

____

____

4. List one challenge you are working on

____

____

____

____

____

____

5. List a new positive attitude you have found for yourself.

____

____

____

____

____

____

6. List three rewards you have given yourself (Nonfood rewards)
   Make 6 copies, Do 1 a week for 6 weeks.

Be Yourself.
Accept Yourself.
Value Yourself.
Forgive Yourself.
Bless Yourself.
Express Yourself.
Trust Yourself.
Love Yourself.
Empower Yourself.

The connection between codependency and recovery is like a puzzle where one piece relies on the other. Codependency and recovery are intertwined in a way that shows how they impact each other. Codependency is when someone relies too much on another person for their sense of identity or well-being. It's like having all your puzzle pieces mixed up and depending on someone else to put them together for you. This can be a challenge because it might mean you're not fully taking care of yourself.

Now, recovery is like finding and putting together those puzzle pieces on your own. It's about becoming stronger and healthier, both mentally and emotionally. When someone is on the journey of recovery, they learn to rely on themselves more and build a better understanding of who they are.

The interesting part is that codependency can be a roadblock to recovery. If you're always depending on someone else, it can be hard to focus on your own growth. On the flip side, going through the recovery process can help break the patterns of codependency. So, the relationship between codependency and recovery is like a dance. When you start learning the steps of recovery, you may find yourself stepping away from codependency. It's a journey of self-discovery and independence, where each step forward in recovery is a step towards breaking free from the ties of codependency.

Codependency often stems from unhealthy or dysfunctional relationships. It occurs when one person excessively relies on another for their emotional needs and sense of identity. In a codependent relationship, there might be a lack of boundaries, with one person's well-being becoming overly intertwined with the other people. This can lead to a cycle of seeking validation and approval from the partner, often at the expense of one's own needs and desires.

People with codependent tendencies may find it challenging to establish and maintain healthy boundaries. They may prioritize others' needs above their own, leading to a diminished sense of self. This reliance on external validation can hinder personal growth and self-discovery.

Recovery, whether from addiction, mental health challenges, or other life struggles, involves a process of self-discovery and healing. It requires us to take a closer look at ourselves, our behaviors, and our relationships. In the context of codependency, the journey of recovery becomes intertwined with breaking free from these unhealthy relationship patterns.

In the recovery process, individuals learn the importance of self-reliance. This involves developing the ability to meet one's emotional needs and make decisions independently. Breaking the cycle of codependency involves shifting the focus from seeking external validation to building internal strength and resilience. Recovery often involves establishing and maintaining healthy boundaries in relationships. This is a crucial aspect of breaking free from codependency. Learning to say no when necessary, expressing one's needs, and respecting the boundaries of others contribute to building healthier and more balanced relationships.

Codependency can erode self-esteem as individuals may derive their sense of worth from external sources. This can be counteracted by practicing the self-esteem program. Recovery involves the cultivation of self-esteem and self-love. This process encourages individuals to recognize and celebrate their intrinsic value, independent of external validation. Recovery is a journey of self-discovery. As individuals progress in their recovery, they often rediscover and embrace their own identity. This process contrasts with the codependent dynamic, where one's identity may become entangled with that of another person.

The relationship between codependency and recovery is a transformative journey. Recovery provides the tools and insights needed to untangle oneself from unhealthy relationship patterns, fostering personal growth, and the development of healthier connections with others. Breaking free from codependency is a significant milestone in the recovery process, leading to increased self-awareness, resilience, and a more authentic sense of self.

Codependency Cycle				
Part	**In Balance**	**Out of Balance**	**Old Role**	**New Role**
Rescuer	Caring Giving Nurturing	Self-Sacrifices Enabler Manipulative	Caretaker "Saves Others"	Caregiver Supports Inner Child Willing To Be Responsible
Victim	Acknowledges Vulnerability "Acknowledges Pain" "Admits Powerlessness" Willing to Grieve Asks for help	Addicted To Suffering Needy Hopeless Clinging Passive Paranoid	Sufferer Helpless Blamer Needs Crises Pessimistic Resents	Seeks Help From Within
Persecutor/ Protector	Protects Self Sets Boundaries Assertive	Vindictive Abusive Vengeful Violent Blaming	Persecutor	Protector

Exercises that aid self-awareness and move you into choices.

EPC Exercise

1. Enter self-hypnosis to communicate with someone you need to complete communication with. This person can be living or dead.
2. Meet with the individual or individuals and say anything you need to. Have a real dialogue as you ping-pong back and forth between yourself and the other person dialoguing about an issue.
3. Work towards resolution of your issues.
4. Deepen for suggestions and visualizations based on resolution. Use I statements "I now know my father love me. I am confidently letting go of the past"
5. Do a Mental Rehearsal of new behaviors. Infuse with positive emotions. Return to normal consciousness.

Run and Change Exercise

1. Go into self-hypnosis and observe a past event which creates problems for you.
2. Talk to your Inner Self about how to heal this event.
3. Use your imagination to change the event thereby creating a positive resource state... You can use a Dream Metaphor.
4. Deepen for suggestions and visualizations. Imagine yourself being confident and successful in the event. Say to yourself

"Every Day in Every Way Better and Better" or another affirmation.

5. Do a Mental Rehearsal of new behaviors. Infuse with positive emotions. Return to normal consciousness.

Meeting Your Subpersonalities.

With eyes closed, after a very short induction, listen to the following sentences. After accepting the first thing that comes to your consciousness, open your eyes and complete the sentence in writing; Close your eyes again and wait for the next sentence.

1. You should _________________________________
2. Don't trust _________________________________
3. Screw this! Let's _________________________________
4. This is a piece of cake! I can _________________________
5. You know what's fun, is to _________________________
6. My favorite thing is _________________________________
7. I can't _________________________________
8. People always _________________________________
9. In our family, we _________________________________
10. If I don't go by the rules, _________________________

Throughout our life experience, we develop coping strategies in order to help us get our needs met. These needs include the need to survive, and the need to be loved and accepted. Beneath each repressed or fragmented inner aspect is an unmet need. As we were growing up, we observed each situation, then created a way of being with it that least threatened our survival/acceptance. We developed an "Identity" which corresponded to the situation.

As we were growing up, we internalized many of the messages we heard (or perceived) about who we are. We disowned and repressed some of these to the shadows in fear that "if you really knew me, you wouldn't like me." Others became fragmented and intensified in the hopes that "when I'm like this, I get praise, and you like me."

Patterns of coping become "instead" behavior to the present feeling we are experiencing which we've learned is either unacceptable or threatening to be getting our needs met.

Coping Exercise

1. Instead of feeling lonely, I _________________________________
2. Instead of feeling angry, I _________________________________
3. Instead of feeling sad, I _________________________________
4. Instead of feeling scared, I _________________________________
5. Instead of feeling empty, I _________________________________
6. Instead of feeling anxious, I _________________________________
7. Instead of feeling depressed, I _________________________________

Having noted your "instead" behaviors, for each one complete the following. Go inside for a moment and ask each part what beliefs it holds that motivate these behaviors. Where did you get these beliefs? (Mom, Dad, church, teacher, etc. How have these beliefs and "instead" behaviors saved your life? How have they caused harm? What would you like to believe instead? What would be different if you believed these new beliefs? What scares you about believing differently than you have in the past? What are you afraid you'll lose? What are you afraid you'll gain? What are you afraid you'll have to do if you change your "instead" behavior? What might happen? Take the time to really think about these things. Then journal about your experience.

Shadow Selves Hold the Key to Addiction Recovery

Carl Jung wrote, "The shadow is a moral problem that challenges the whole ego personality, for no one can become conscious of the shadow without considerable moral effort. To become conscious of it involves recognizing the dark aspects of the personality as present and real. This act is the essential condition for any kind of self-knowledge, and is therefore, as a rule meets with considerable resistance. Indeed, self-knowledge as a psychotherapeutic measure frequently requires much painstaking work. These resistances are usually bound up with projections, which are not recognized as such, and their recognition is a moral achievement beyond the ordinary.

No matter how obvious it may be to the neutral observer that this is a matter of projections; there is little hope that we will easy perceive this ourselves. We must be convinced that we throw a very long shadow before we are willing to withdraw our emotionally toned projections from their object." Our projections change the world into a mirror of our own "unknown" self/personality. The tragedy of projection is that we do not do this consciously. We are unconscious of the illusions we have placed on our environment. The Journey of Recovery requires our willingness to truly see ourselves, to let go of the past and to design our lives through conscious choices.

(Insert Graphic # 15)

1. Amplify . . . Through suggestion
2. Entering . . . Deepening
3. Becoming . . . Identification

Working Through Resistance

Always create safety for yourself by surround yourself with a energy field of white light. Connection with your Soul, Spiritual Guides, Higher Power or Inner Self. These are the These are your Spiritual Resources. Use what term is most comfortable for you. The safer and more spiritually connected you feel the less resistance you will have.

Causes of Resistance

1. You avoid or disapproves of the expression of feeling or emotions.
2. You feel shamed or guilty.
3. You are afraid of your memories.
4. Use your connection with your Spiritual Resources to guide you.

Wall and Guard Technique

Write about something that is blocking you:

____

____

____

____

____

1. Imagine a wall
2. Follow the wall
3. Find a gate and guard
4. Talk to the guard
5. Become the guard
6. As the guard chose to go through the gate!

Journal feelings and emotions:

____

____

____

____

____

To truly understand yourself, it's essential to step away from the roles you often find yourself playing. This means taking a moment to connect with your inner spirituality—the part of you that goes beyond the everyday tasks and responsibilities. It's like peeling away the layers to reveal the real and essential you. This will help you explore and uncover how you envision different aspects of your life. Think of your life as a wheel with various areas: relationships, work, hobbies, and more. You can begin visualizing how you want each section of this wheel to look and feel.

To make this process more concrete, I have created a survey I the next chapter. It's a set of questions designed to help you clearly define your ideal life. These questions encourage you to think deeply about your values, desires, and aspirations. This exercise is crucial because it paints a vivid picture of what your best life looks like. The beauty of this journey is that it leads you to a space where you can be your authentic self. It's about aligning your life with your true values and aspirations. Imagine being in a place where your actions, decisions, and relationships reflect the real you—no masks, no pretending. The empowering message here is that you are not bound by your past or current circumstances.

The idea is that you can shape your future. By changing your mindset—how you perceive yourself and your possibilities—you can profoundly impact your life. It's a reminder that you are in control of the narrative, and every small change in your thinking can lead to significant changes in your life. The phrase "change your mind, change your life" encapsulates the transformative power of your thoughts. By shifting your perspective, you have the potential to transform your experiences. This is not about changing who you are but understanding and embracing your true self, leading to a life that aligns with your deepest values and aspirations. In essence, the journey to a recovered life involves self-discovery, visualization, and a conscious effort to live authentically. Remember, you have the ability to shape your future—one thought, one decision, one choice at a time.

Copy the link in your browser and download your Letting Go of the Past MP3
http://zoilitagrant.net/media/files/18Letting_Go_Past/dlcd18.htm

CHAPTER 6

FROM BURNOUT TO BRILLIANCE

Imagine feeling exhausted, stressed, and overwhelmed, like you've been running on a treadmill that never stops. This is what burnout feels like, and it's something many people, including students like us, may experience. Burnout is not just being tired after a busy day; it's a deep, persistent feeling of physical and emotional exhaustion.

Picture this: You have a mountain of work, and personal activities piling up. You're juggling deadlines, trying to keep up with friends, family, and everything else life throws your way. Slowly, the energy that once fueled your passion for work, for learning, and for life starts to dwindle, and you find yourself mentally and emotionally drained.

Burnout doesn't happen overnight. It's a gradual process that creeps up when we neglect our well-being and push ourselves too hard without taking breaks. The pressure to excel, participate in numerous activities, and maintain a bustling social life can build up until it becomes overwhelming.

Symptoms of burnout can manifest in various ways. You might notice a lack of motivation, difficulty concentrating, and a sense of detachment from your once-beloved activities. Physical signs, such as headaches and trouble sleeping, can also be indicators that your mind and body are struggling to cope with the demands placed on them.

It's crucial to recognize the signs of burnout and take steps to prevent it. This means finding a balance between school, extracurriculars, and personal time. Setting realistic goals, learning to say no when needed, and incorporating relaxation techniques into your routine can make a significant difference in preserving your mental and emotional well-being.

Remember, it's okay to ask for help. Talk to a friend, a coach, or a trusted mentor if you're feeling overwhelmed. Taking care of your mental health is just as important as tackling your responsibilities. By recognizing the signs of burnout early and making self-care a priority, you can navigate the challenges of life more successfully.

Burnout is more than just feeling tired: it's a state of chronic physical and emotional exhaustion brought on by prolonged stress and overwork. As you navigate the challenges of life, it's crucial to understand the signs of burnout. One of the early indicators of burnout is a noticeable decline in motivation. You might find it increasingly difficult to muster the enthusiasm you once had for your work or extracurricular pursuits. This lack of motivation can quickly spiral into feelings of frustration and disinterest, making it challenging to stay engaged in your work and personal endeavors. The symptoms of burnout to prevent it from taking a toll on your well-being.

Concentration becomes another casualty of burnout. As the demands on your time increase, you may struggle to focus on tasks, leading to decreased productivity and a sense of being overwhelmed. This mental fog can hinder your ability to absorb information efficiently.

Physical symptoms can also manifest when burnout takes hold. Frequent headaches disrupted sleep patterns, and even stomachaches might become part of your daily routine. Your body is sending distress signals, indicating that the stress and pressure are affecting not only your mind but your physical well-being as well.

Moreover, burnout often brings about a sense of detachment. Activities that once brought joy may now feel like burdens. The hobbies and interests that used to be your escape may lose their allure. This emotional detachment can strain relationships and contribute to a growing sense of isolation.

Preventing burnout involves recognizing these signs and taking proactive steps to address them. Establishing a realistic schedule that includes breaks and downtime is crucial. Learning to prioritize tasks and say no, when necessary, can help manage the overwhelming demands on your plate.

Equally important is incorporating self-care practices into your routine. This could include activities like meditation, exercise, or simply taking a moment to unwind with a book or a favorite hobby. Seeking support from mentors, teachers, friends, or family members can also be a valuable resource in navigating the challenges without succumbing to burnout.

Remember, recognizing and addressing burnout is a form of strength, not weakness. Taking care of your mental and emotional well-being is an essential aspect of achieving long-term success. By acknowledging the signs of burnout and implementing strategies to manage stress, you'll be better equipped to navigate the stresses of your current life and beyond.

As we move away from burnout to creating success in our lives, it is important to define what success is. Success is a subjective and multifaceted concept that varies from person to person. It is often defined by the achievement of goals, the fulfillment of aspirations, or the attainment of a desired outcome. Success can manifest in various aspects of life, including personal, professional, academic, or even interpersonal realms.

For some individuals, success may be closely tied to career accomplishments, such as climbing the corporate ladder, starting a successful business, or achieving recognition in a particular field. Others may find success in personal relationships, such as building a loving family or fostering meaningful connections with friends and community. Academic success is another dimension, often measured by achieving educational goals, obtaining degrees, or mastering a particular subject. For some, success might be linked to personal development and continuous learning.

Furthermore, success is not solely about external achievements; it can also encompass internal growth and well-being. Achieving a sense of fulfillment, contentment, and inner peace can be seen as a form of success. This may involve overcoming personal challenges, developing resilience, and cultivating a positive success mindset.

Ultimately, success is a dynamic and evolving concept. It is deeply personal and influenced by individual values, priorities, and life circumstances. The pursuit of success is often a journey rather than a destination, and people may redefine their understanding of success at different stages of their lives. Your mindset is a set of your beliefs that shape how you perceive of and understand the world and yourself. It influences how you think, feel, and behave in any given situation. It means that what you believe about yourself impacts your ability to have success or failure.

Your mindset can influence how you behave in the different situations you face in your life. For example, as people encounter different situations, their mind triggers a specific mindset that then directly impacts their behavior in that situation. Mindset is everything. It is like a TV channel that you tune into. Most commonly people have fixed or growth mindsets. Growth mindsets open you to potential and growth. They create the opportunity for maximum potential and success in life. While mindsets are generally created in childhood, you can change and create growth mindsets through conscious choices. By developing greater self-esteem and using self-hypnosis and positive self-talk, you can shift your mindset. Your mindset determines how you cope with your experiences of life.

In the early 1990s, coaches started using Life Design techniques to inspire people like you to achieve greater success. These coaches believed that people had strengths, abilities, and skills that they might not fully recognize. They thought that people had already tried to find solutions to their life challenges but didn't give themselves enough credit. Life Design aims to help you to tap into your own resources and future potential, by focusing on how you want your life to be.

In Success Hypnotic Coaching, like I do, I want you to be thinking about your future possibilities. Instead of dwelling on problems, I want you to ask yourself questions like, "How would I like things to be different?" Part of why I wrote this book is because I believe in guiding you through positive changes. I think you are an expert in your challenges, and I want to help you create practical solutions.

The "miracle question," developed in the 1980s in Solution Focused Therapy, is often used. It asks you to imagine waking up to a miraculous solution to your problems and to describe the first noticeable change. This helps you to map out your journey to a solution without dwelling on why the challenges exist.

Moving from Solution Focused Therapy to the Life Design presented is a natural transition from therapy to coaching. Once you connect with your Future Self, who has overcome current challenges and serves as an internal guide, you can begin to design your life. You can learn about the Keys to Your Ideal Life, the Five Laws of Success, and create your own Wheel of Life. Before the journey to find the Future Self, I have some survey material to fill out: the Signature Strength Survey, Values

Clarification, Discovering Needs, Clarifying Your Passions, and Defining Your Ideal Life exercise. These exercises will dramatically improve your self-awareness and combined with your Inner Wisdom can set concrete goals to move towards your Ideal Life.

Life Design is a powerful approach, evolving as a response to the growing need to inspire individuals towards greater success. At its core, Life Design operates on the belief that every individual possesses inherent strengths, abilities, and untapped resources. I know most of you have probably made attempts to navigate life challenges but may not fully recognize or credit yourselves for your capabilities.

The fundamental philosophy of Life Design centers around connecting with your own reservoir of resources and untapped potentials. You have now walked the Recovery Steps. Although Recovery often continues for a while, you have less to go than you have already come. Let Life Design direct your attention toward the future. It is time to actively envision and shape the lives you desire. I am here to help you to focused on future possibilities and aspirations.

Instead of dwelling on the issues, ask yourself thought-provoking questions like, "How would I like things to be different?". The underlying belief is that change is a constant, and we need the guidance of being steered through a framework of positive transformations. There is a lot you can do with the exercises in this book. I also highly recommend getting a hypnotic coach. I have worked with a coach for about 15 years.

A significant tool within the Life Design is the "miracle question," borrowed from Solution Focused Therapy. This question invites you to imagine a scenario where your problems are miraculously solved, setting the stage for constructive thought on potential solutions without getting bogged down by the origins of challenges. Life Design is not just a coaching technique but a holistic approach that empowers you to take charge of your lives, leverage your strengths, and actively shape a future aligned with your aspirations. It encourages a shift from focusing on problems to envisioning and creating a life filled with purpose and fulfillment.

Keys to the Ideal Life (Keys open doors)

1. Realize you create your reality.
2. Get a clear picture of what you want to create.
3. Remove the blocks and limitations.
4. Develop a plan to take you from where you are to where you want to be.
5. Reprogram yourself for success.

Five Laws of Success

1. **The first law is the Law of Attraction and Vibration:** the energy and actions that we put out into the world is the energy and actions that we receive back. That is what Karma is about. Our

thoughts, feelings, and actions attract to us what we receive in the world. Outer reality does indeed mirror what is inside of us. It's all about energy. You must be a vibrational match to what you want to attract.

2. **The second law is the Law of Intention:** setting intentions, clearly and are essential in creating lives that we truly enjoy. The more clearly that intentions are set, the more easily we can create them.

3. **The third law is the Law of Celebration and Gratitude:** cultivating an attitude of gratitude and counting your blessings creates the heart space for more blessings to come into your life.

4. **The fourth law is the Law of Receptivity:** our ability to have a joyous and abundant life is only limited by our capacity to receive. It is important to increase your ability to receive.

5. **The fifth law is the Law of Involvement:** our lives are our responsibility. Do your own part. Involve yourself in the process of creating your life. Remember it is your life!

Learn Your Strengths (Make this section look clean)
Authentic Happiness Signature Strength Survey
by Martin Seligman, Ph.D.

<u>Wisdom & Knowledge:</u>

1. **CURIOSITY / INTEREST IN THE WORLD**

a) The statement **"I am always curious about the world"** is

- Very much like me **5**   - Like me **4**   Neutral **3**
- Unlike me **2**   Very much unlike me **1**

b) **"I am easily bored"** is

- Very much like me **1**   - Like me **2**   Neutral **3**
- Unlike me **4**   Very much unlike me **5**

Total your score for these two items and write here: ______________
(This is your curiosity score.)

2. **LOVE OF LEARNING**

a) The statement **"I am thrilled when I learn something new"** is

- Very much like me **5**   - Like me **4**   Neutral **3**
            - Unlike me **2**   Very much unlike me **1**

b) **"I never go out of my way to visit museums or other educational sites"** is

- Very much like me **1**   - Like me **2**   Neutral **3**
            - Unlike me **4**   Very much unlike me **5**

Total your score for these two items and write here: __________
(This is your love of learning score.)

3. **JUDGEMENT / CRITICAL THINKING / OPEN-MINDEDNESS**

a) The statement **"When the topic calls for it, I can be a highly rational thinker** is

- Very much like me **1**   - Like me **2**   Neutral **3**
            - Unlike me **4**   Very much unlike me **5**

b) **"I tend to make snap judgments"** is

- Very much like me **1**   - Like me **2**   Neutral **3**
            - Unlike me **4**   Very much unlike me **5**

Total your score for these two items and write here: ______________
(This is your judgment score.)

4. **INGENUITY / ORIGINALITY / PRACTICAL INTELLIGENCE / STREET SMARTS**

a) **"I like to think of new ways to do things"** is

- Very much like me **1**   - Like me **2**   Neutral **3**
          - Unlike me **4**   Very much unlike me **5**

b) "**Most of my friends are more imaginative than I am**" is

- Very much like me **1**   - Like me **2**   Neutral **3**
          - Unlike me **4**   Very much unlike me **5**

Total your score for these two items and write here: _______________
(This is your ingenuity score.)

5. **SOCIAL INTELLIGENCE / PERSONAL INTELLIGENCE / EMOTIONAL – INTELLIGENCE**

a) **"No matter what the social situation, I am able to fit in"** is

- Very much like me **5**   - Like me **4**   Neutral **3**
          - Unlike me **2**   Very much unlike me **1**

b) "**I am not very good at sensing what other people are feeling**" is

- Very much like me **1**   - Like me **2**   Neutral **3**
          - Unlike me **4**   Very much unlike me **5**

Total your score for these two items and write here: _______________
(This is your social intelligence score.)

6. **PERSPECTIVE**

a) **"I am always able to look at things and see the big picture"** is

- Very much like me **5**   - Like me **4**   Neutral **3**
- Unlike me **2**   Very much unlike me **1**

b) "Others rarely come to me for advice" is

- Very much like me **1**   - Like me **2**   Neutral **3**
- Unlike me **4**   Very much unlike me **5**

Total your score for these two items and write here: ______________
(This is your perspective score.)

<u>Courage:</u>

7. **VALOR AND BRAVERY**

a) "I have taken frequent stands in the face of strong opposition" is

- Very much like me **5**   - Like me **4**   Neutral **3**
- Unlike me **2**   Very much unlike me **1**

<u>b</u>) "Pain and disappointment often get the better of me" is

- Very much like me **1**   - Like me **2**   Neutral **3**
- Unlike me **4**   Very much unlike me **5**

Total your score for these two items and write here: ______________
(This is your valor score.)

8. **PERSEVERANCE / INDUSTRY / DILIGENCE**

a) "I always finish what I start" is

- Very much like me **5**   - Like me **4**   Neutral **3**
- Unlike me **2**   Very much unlike me **1**

b) "I get sidetracked when I work" is

- Very much like me **1**   - Like me **2**   Neutral **3**
- Unlike me **4**   Very much unlike me **5**

Total your score for these two items and write here: ___________
(This is your perseverance score.)

9. INTEGRITY / GENUINENESS / HONESTY

a) **"I always keep my promises"** is

- Very much like me **5**   - Like me **4**   Neutral **3**
- Unlike me **2**   Very much unlike me **1**

b) **"My friends never tell me I am down to earth"** is

- Very much like me **1**   - Like me **2**   Neutral **3**
- Unlike me **4**   Very much unlike me **5**

Total your score for these two items and write here: ___________
(This is your integrity score.)

<u>**Humanity & Love:**</u>

10. KINDNESS AND GENEROSITY

a) **"I have voluntarily helped a neighbor in the last month"** is

- Very much like me **5**   - Like me **4**   Neutral **3**
- Unlike me **2**   Very much unlike me **1**

b) **"I am rarely as excited about the good fortune of others as I am about my own"** is

- Very much like me **1**   - Like me **2**   Neutral **3**
- Unlike me **4**   Very much unlike me **5**

Total your score for these two items and write here: _______________
(This is your kindness score.)

11. 11. LOVING AND ALLOWING ONESELF TO BE LOVED

a) **"There are people in my life who care as much about my feelings and well-being as they do about their own"** is

- Very much like me **5**   - Like me **4**   Neutral **3**
  - Unlike me **2**   Very much unlike me **1**

b) **"I have trouble accepting love from others"** is

- Very much like me **1**   - Like me **2**   Neutral **3**
  - Unlike me **4**   Very much unlike me **5**

Total your score for these two items and write here: _______________
(This is your loving and being loved score.)

<u>Justice:</u>

12. CITIZENSHIP / DUTY / TEAMWORK / LOYALTY

a) **"I am work at my best when I am in a group"** is

- Very much like me **5**   - Like me **4**   Neutral **3**
  - Unlike me **2**   Very much unlike me **1**

b) **"I hesitate to sacrifice myself interest for the benefit for groups I am in"** is

- Very much like me **1**   - Like me **2**   Neutral **3**
  - Unlike me **4**   Very much unlike me **5**

Total your score for these two items and write here: _______________
(This is your citizenship score.)

13. FAIRNESS AND EQUITY

a) **"I treat all people equally regardless of who they might be"** is

- Very much like me **5**   - Like me **4**   Neutral **3**
- Unlike me **2**   Very much unlike me **1**

b) **"If I do not like someone, it is difficult for me to treat him or her fairly"** is

- Very much like me **1**   - Like me **2**   Neutral **3**
- Unlike me **4**   Very much unlike me **5**

Total your score for these two items and write here: ______________
(This is your fairness score.)

14. LEADERSHIP

a) **"I can always get people to do things together without nagging them"**

- Very much like me **5**   - Like me **4**   Neutral **3**
- Unlike me **2**   Very much unlike me **1**

b) **"I am not very good at planning group activities"** is

- Very much like me **1**   - Like me **2**   Neutral **3**
- Unlike me **4**   Very much unlike me **5**

Total your score for these two items and write here: ______________
(This is your leadership score.

<u>Temperance:</u>

15. SELF-CONTROL

a) **"I control my emotions"** is

- Very much like me **5**   - Like me **4**   Neutral **3**
- Unlike me **2**   Very much unlike me **1**

b) **"I can rarely stay on a diet"** is

- Very much like me **1**   - Like me **2**   Neutral **3**
- Unlike me **4**   Very much unlike me **5**

Total your score for these two items and write here: ______________
(This is your self-control score

16. **PRUDENCE / DISCRECTION / CAUTION**

a) **"I avoid activities that are physically dangerous"** is

- Very much like me **5**   - Like me **4**   Neutral **3**
- Unlike me **2**   Very much unlike me **1**

b) **"I sometime make poor choices in friendships and relationships"** is

- Very much like me **1**   - Like me **2**   Neutral **3**
- Unlike me **4**   Very much unlike me **5**

Total your score for these two items and write here: ______________
(This is your prudence score.)

17. **HUMILITY AND MODESTY**

a) **"I change the subject when people pay me compliments"** is

- Very much like me **5**   - Like me **4**   Neutral **3**
- Unlike me **2**   Very much unlike me **1**

b) **"I often talk about my accomplishments"** is

- Very much like me **1**   - Like me **2**   Neutral **3**

- Unlike me **4**   Very much unlike me **5**

Total your score for these two items and write here: ______________
(This is your humility score.

<u>Transcendence:</u>

18. APPRECIATION OF BEAUTY AND EXCELLENCE

a) **"In the last month I have been thrilled by excellence in music, art, drama, film, sport, science or mathematics"** is

- Very much like me **5**   - Like me **4**   Neutral **3**
    - Unlike me **2**   Very much unlike me **1**

b) **"I have not created anything of beauty in the last year"** is

- Very much like me **1**   - Like me **2**   Neutral **3**
    - Unlike me **4**   Very much unlike me **5**

Total your score for these two items and write here: ______________
(This is your appreciation of beauty score.)

19. GRATITUDE

a) **"I always say thank you, even for little things"** is

- Very much like me **5**   - Like me **4**   Neutral **3**
    - Unlike me **2**   Very much unlike me **1**

b) **"I rarely stop and count my blessings"** is

- Very much like me **1**   - Like me **2**   Neutral **3**
    - Unlike me **4**   Very much unlike me **5**

Total your score for these two items and write here: ______________
(This is your gratitude score.)

20. **HOPE / OPTIMISIM / FUTURE-MINDEDNESS**

a) **"I always look on the bright side"** is

- Very much like me **5**   - Like me **4**   Neutral **3**
           - Unlike me **2**   Very much unlike me **1**

b) **"I rarely have a well-thought-out plan for what I want to do"** is

- Very much like me **1**   - Like me **2**   Neutral **3**
           - Unlike me **4**   Very much unlike me **5**

Total your score for these two items and write here: ______________
(This is your optimism score.)

21. **SPIRITUALITY / SENSE OF PURPOSE / FAITH / RELIGIOUSNESS**

a) **"My life has a strong purpose"** is

- Very much like me **5**   - Like me **4**   Neutral **3**
           - Unlike me **2**   Very much unlike me **1**

b) **"I do not have a calling in life"** is

- Very much like me **1**   - Like me **2**   Neutral **3**
           - Unlike me **4**   Very much unlike me **5**

Total your score for these two items and write here: ______________
(This is your spirituality score.)

22. **22. FORGIVENESS AND MERCY**

a) **"I always let bygones be bygones"** is

- Very much like me **5**   - Like me **4**   Neutral **3**
        - Unlike me **2**   Very much unlike me **1**

b) **"I always try to get even"** is

- Very much like me **1**   - Like me **2**   Neutral **3**
        - Unlike me **4**   Very much unlike me **5**

Total your score for these two items and write here: ______________
(This is your forgiveness score.)

23. PLAYFULNESS AND HUMOR

a) **"I always mix work and play as much as possible"** is

- Very much like me **5**   - Like me **4**   Neutral **3**
        - Unlike me **2**   Very much unlike me **1**

b) **"I rarely say funny things"** is

- Very much like me **1**   - Like me **2**   Neutral **3**
        - Unlike me **4**   Very much unlike me **5**

Total your score for these two items and write here: ______________
(This is your humor score.)

24. ZEST / PASSION / ENTHUSIASM

a) **"I throw myself into everything I do"** is

- Very much like me **5**   - Like me **4**   Neutral **3**
        - Unlike me **2**   Very much unlike me **1**

b) **"I mope a lot"** is

- Very much like me **1**   - Like me **2**   Neutral **3**

- Unlike me **4**   Very much unlike me **5**

Total your score for these two items and write here: ___________
(This is your zest score.)

Adapted from the Values-In-Action Classification of Strengths and Virtues, developed under the direction of Christopher Peterson and Martin Seligman.

Total the scores. Focus on and develop your strengths. (Make sure all lines are straight)

WISDOM AND KNOWLEDGE

1. Curiosity ___________
2. Love of learning___________
3. Judgment ___________
4. Ingenuity ___________
5. Social intelligence ___________
6. Perspective ___________

COURAGE

7. Valor ___________
8. Perseverance ___________
9. Integrity ___________

HUMANITY AND LOVE

10. Kindness ___________
11. Loving ___________

JUSTICE

12. Citizenship ___________
13. Fairness ___________
14. Leadership ___________

TEMPERANCE

15. Self-control _________________
16. Prudence _________________
17. Humility _________________

TRANSCENDENCE

18. Appreciation of beauty _________________
19. Gratitude _________________
20. Hope _________________
21. Spirituality _________________
22. Forgiveness _________________
23. Humor _________________
24. Zest _________________

Clarify Your Values

Pick your top 5 ideal values (the way you want it to be) It there is a value that you want to enhance put a star on it

Loyalty / Ethics	Sports and Hobbies	Physical Health
Independence	Power	Emotional Health
Physical Appearance	Beautiful Surroundings /Owning Nice Things	Openness
Creativity	Financial Security	Pleasure
Generosity	Sexuality	Career
Education	Spirituality	Parenting
Justice	Success & Achievement	Coupleship
	Recognition & Social Acceptance	

Discover Your Passions

Passions are key to finding a sense of Life Purpose. They are elements which help us to find a sense of flow regeneration in the things that we do. I highly recommend a book called the Passion Test by Janet Bray Attwood and Chris Attwood for an easy system for working with your Passions to create a Passion Filled Life. Begin with ten things that you feel passionate about and then work down to your Top Five Passions.

Ten Things I Feel Passionate About:

1. ____
1. ____
2. ____
3. ____
4. ____
5. ____
6. ____
7. ____
8. ____

Go back and put a * next to your top five

My Top Five Passions:

1. ____
2. ____
3. ____
4. ____
5. ____

**"Whenever you are faced with a decision, choice or opportunity, always choose in favor of your passions!"
Janet Bray Atwood – The Passion Test
http://www.thepassiontest.com**

Identify Your Needs

We often forget the difference between having needs and being needy. The truth is that we all have needs, they are normal and natural. The problem is that most of us do not allow ourselves to acknowledge our needs exist. When we believe that we need to deny our needs, they go underground and cause us problems in our lives. Abraham Maslow said every human being has a Hierarchy of Needs. He created a model for identifying human needs. In this model, human beings move up levels as their basic needs are met.

I have learned that needs must be met for a person to do their best. Unmet needs create distractions. Needs are affected by situations in your life. Needs are different from wants and desires. It is important to acknowledge that you have needs. If you have trouble identifying your needs, that is a very important message. You can find unmet needs by tracking some of your emotions. When a need is not being met you may feel frustrated, fearful, disappointed, hurt, and angry. Track the patterns of your charged emotions and you will find the needs. Another excellent technique is to work with your committee.

What are you five greatest needs at this time in your life? Start with ten and then work down to Top Five Needs.

My Top Ten Needs Are:

1. ____
2. ____
3. ____
4. ____
5. ____
6. ____
7. ____
8. ____
9. ____
10. ____

Go back and put a * next to your top five.

Prioritize Your Top Five Needs:

1. ____
2. ____
3. ____
4. ____
5. ____

Create a scale 0-5 and compare to Your Wheel of Life

    0   Need not present in this area.

    1   Need not met.

    5   Need met completely.

Use this Needs Assessment with the Wheel of Life. Our needs can drive us until we learn how to drive and direct them. We need to ask ourselves if we are meeting our needs in the easiest and healthiest ways.

What Needs are Not Getting Met?

What Can You Do to Better Get Them Met?

What Will You Do first?

When will You Begin?

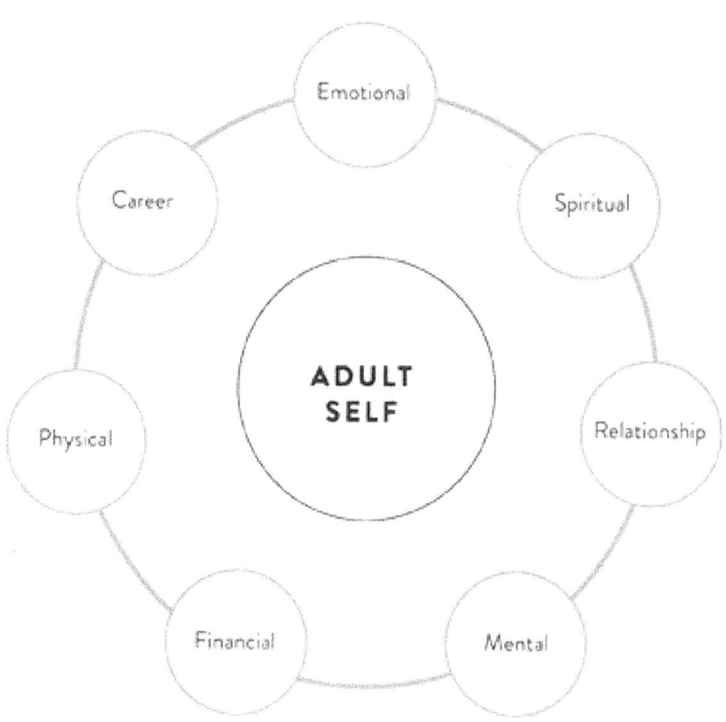

Designing Your Ideal Life

Emotional Life:

How will you feel in your Ideal Life? How will you express your full range of emotions in that Ideal Life?

____

____

____

____

____

____

Relationship and Family Life:

Describe your ideal loving relationship and family life. List the qualities that you would like to have in your mate. What size of family, type of coupleship? What kind of friends will you have? What kind of groups will you get involved with?

____

____

____

____

____

Mental Life:

What do you want to do with your mind? What kind of things stimulate you? What would you like to study? What are the things that keep you intellectually stimulated?

____

____

____

____

____

Physical Life:

What is your Ideal Weight or level of Fitness? How do you eat in your Ideal Life?

What kind of physical exercise do you do in your Ideal Life?

____

____

____

____

____

Financial:

What are your finances like in your ideal life? How much money do you make?

What is your standard of living in your Ideal Life? Be detailed and specific.

____

____

____

____

____

Career:

What is your ideal career? What do you love doing that gives you a sense of pleasure and purpose?

____

____

____

____

____

Spiritual Life:

Spiritually how do you connect with your own sense of the Divine? What is your philosophy of life? What is your authentic self really like?

____

____

____

____

____

It's essential to have a clear sense of life purpose because it serves as a guiding force, offering direction and meaning to one's journey. This sense of purpose plays a crucial role in decision-making, acting as a compass that helps individuals align their choices with their values and long-term goals. When you understand your life purpose, it becomes a powerful motivator, fueling passion and dedication to your pursuits.

Moreover, a defined life purpose contributes to resilience in the face of challenges. Life can be demanding, but knowing the greater meaning behind your efforts provides strength, aiding in overcoming obstacles and bouncing back from setbacks. This resilience, in turn, contributes to positive mental health, reducing stress, and fostering emotional well-being.

A sense of purpose extends its impact to interpersonal dynamics, connecting individuals with like-minded people who share similar values and goals. This fosters a supportive community and facilitates the development of meaningful relationships. Additionally, understanding one's life purpose leads to increased satisfaction in life, allowing individuals to appreciate the journey and find joy in their accomplishments, both big and small.

The significance of having a life purpose becomes evident in goal setting. It enables individuals to set meaningful objectives that contribute to their larger purpose, making their efforts more rewarding and purposeful. Furthermore, having a life purpose often involves contributing to something beyond oneself, whether through helping others, making a positive impact in the community, or pursuing a passion. This element of contribution adds depth and meaning to life, creating a positive ripple effect on the world around you.

In summary, a sense of life purpose functions as a roadmap, providing direction, motivation, and a framework for building a meaningful and fulfilling existence.,It helps you to find your brilliance.

Keys to Finding Your Life Purpose

- Realize that you create your purpose.
- Get a clear picture of what gives you a sense of purpose.
- Create a Statement of Life Purpose:

- Remove the blocks and limitations. (What Stands Between You and your Life Purpose?)
- Program your mind for success:
- Write an affirmation which supports your Life Purpose.

An Affirmation:

- Is a positive statement
- Is stated in the present tense
- Uses few words—packs more punch
  Is repeated daily.

Write Your Life Purpose Statement:

Now I am going to tell you a story. Some of my stories are true, and some contain truth.

Once upon a time, a long time ago, a bustling zoo in the southern lands was home to a colony of polar bears. These majestic creatures endured cramped conditions within the confines of the zoo. Then, on a fateful day, the zookeeper, decided to construct a paradise for the polar bears. So, all the bears were put in cages and taken to the edge of the zoo while the work on the paradise was being done. Within the confines of their cages, the bears began a relentless ritual of pacing, their massive bodies traversing a meager 7 feet by 14 feet space. Back and forth, up and down, they paced ceaselessly as the laborious construction of their promised paradise continued.

Days turned into nights, and the bears, trapped in their cages, kept up their rhythmic pacing. The keeper toiled tirelessly, sculpting a haven for the polar bears. A magnificent mountain of snow emerged, offering the bears an opportunity to climb to the top, ski down its slopes, and skate upon a frozen lake. Yet, the bears, confined by the bars of their cages, persisted in their monotonous pacing. The completion of the paradise seemed a distant dream as the bears continued their relentless ritual, 7 feet by 14 feet, pacing all day long.

Finally, the day arrived when the paradise was declared complete. The bears, still ensnared within their cages, were transported to the edge of the newly crafted heaven. With bated breath, the cages were opened, but to the bewilderment of onlookers, the bears continued their pacing within the confines of their cages.

Suddenly a little bird flew out of the sky and landed on the shoulder of one of the polar bears. The bird whispered, "There are no more bars" The polar bear jumped out of her cage and all the other bears followed her. The message was clear, even in the midst of their enclosure, there were no more bars. The bears left their cages, climbed the mountain of snow, skied down the other side and danced for joy on the lake of ice. Now I don't know what this story will mean for you, or what you will take away, but one thing I do know is that there are no more bars! Time to be free. Time to find your brilliance!

Living an intentional life requires us to develop habits of success. Here are six things you can do at home that will help you to continue to let go of your past and move into brilliance of your potential. As with all things, consistency is important.

Develop these six daily personal habits:

- **Begin each day with 5 mins of gratitude.**
- **Meditate/practice mindfulness (this can be walking or sitting)**
- **Review your goals with feelings.**
- **Exercise at least 20 mins.**
- **Plan your day.**
- **Use your breath to manage your stress.**

If you are interested in continuing your work and accelerating your growth, please join our community https://zoilitagrant.com/breakthrough-to-brilliance/

ABOUT THE AUTHOR

Zoilita Grant is founder of a new branch of coaching called **Hypnotic Coaching.** This style of coaching combines the tools and techniques of coaching with the power and punch of hypnosis. graduated from the University of California at Berkeley in the early 1960s. After nearly a decade traveling, spending time in Vancouver, Canada and serving in the US Army, she completed her master's in social work at the University of Texas at El Paso in 1979. Her fascination with hypnosis led her to complete several certifications in hypnosis. After being exposed to coaching in the early 2000s, she completed the foundation training of the International Coach Federation in 2008. Being a lifelong learner, she was certified as a Virtual Coach in 2023. Zoilita is internationally known as an expert in hypnosis and regularly speaks at hypnosis conferences.

Apart from contract work as a drug and alcohol trainer and managing a couple of non-profits, Zoilita has had a continuous private practice, thirty-five years as a psychotherapist and fifteen years as a success hypnotic coach. She has always operated her practice as a small business and has been very successful in California, Colorado, and now internationally on the Internet. Operating the Colorado School of Counselling Hypnotherapy for over 14 years gave Zoilita the opportunity to write twenty-four books on hypnosis, a series of business mastery kits, and to produce a line of neuro-meditations and mediation MP3s. She is actively involved in her local Chamber of Commerce, The Colorado Association of Psychotherapists (which she helped start) and several hypnosis associations. She donates to many non-profits and regularly volunteers with women's organizations.

Zoilita is passionate about helping people live successful and happy lives. After her personal experience of using hypnosis to lose 150 lbs., she believes the subconscious mind is the key to lasting change. She has been actively involved in helping people transform their lives for fifty years. She has seen thousands clear subconscious blocks, shift their mindset, and get real results in achieving their goals. Results don't lie. With this in mind, her goal is to develop easy to use tools to help people change their lives, overcome their challenges and live truly successful happy lives.

For over thirty years, Zoilita had an incredibly happy marriage. She met the love of her life, Rick, in the public library. At the time she was a single Mom with two very small children. She and Rick married and raised the children to becoming successful adults. Rick was her partner in business and in life. He died suddenly in 2014. Out of this tragedy, Zoilita came to believe that the best way to honor him and the love they shared, was a life well lived. Zoilita loves owls, her family and the mountains. She lives in the beautiful house she shared with Rick and her cat Thomas in Longmont, CO.

CONTACT INFORMATION

E-mail: zoilitagrant@gmail.com
Web site: www.breakthroughtobrilliancecoaching.com

Change Your Mind and Change Your Life
A Step-By-Step Guide for Letting Go of Your Past
Material contained is:
© Zoilita Grant 2024

Come and join our online program:
https://breakthroughtobrilliancecoaching.com/

Benefits of the "Breakthrough to Brilliance" online coaching program

1. **Unlock full your potential** by addressing and clearing subconscious blocks that hinder personal and professional growth.
2. **Live a life of abundance,** by focus on overcoming limiting beliefs around money and developing a mindset that attracts wealth and prosperity.
3. **Achieve a harmonious balance** between personal and professional life, relationships, health, and personal growth. Strategies for effective time management and self-care rituals are included.
4. **Experience significant spiritual growth**, as you are guided to connect with your inner selves and a higher power through guided meditations, visualization techniques, and self-reflection exercises.
5. **Zoilita Grant is skilled in invoking insightful thoughts and challenging current mindsets.** The goal is to facilitate a shift

in perception, leading to a renewed sense of purpose and the confidence to pursue one's dreams.

6. **The "Breakthrough to Brilliance Program aims to demystify the concept of financial abundance, making it accessible to all of you.** Through proven strategies and practical tools, limiting beliefs around money are identified and reprogrammed.

7. **The "Breakthrough to Brilliance Program asserts that "results don't lie," pointing to and revealing the success stories of community members who have reached new heights in their** careers, launched successful businesses, and experienced personal growth.

The "Breakthrough to Brilliance Program aims to provide a holistic approach to personal and professional development, encompassing mindset shifts, financial success, life balance, and spiritual growth.

RESOURCES

Hill. N (2016) <u>Think and Grow Rich</u> (An Official Publication of the Napoleon Hill foundation) Paperback – December 13, 2016

Covey, S (2019) <u>The 7 Habits of Highly Effective People </u>SIMON & SCHUSTER

Assagioli, R (1971) <u>Psychosynthesis.</u> Penguin

Bolen, J (1989) <u>Gods in Every Man.</u> New York: Harper & Row

Bolen, J (1989) <u>Goddess in Every Women.</u> New York: Harper & Row

Bradshaw, J (1989) <u>On The Family.</u> Health Communications Inc.

Bradshaw, J (1988) <u>Healing The Shame That Binds You.</u>

Health Communications Inc.

Bradshaw, J (1990) <u>Homecoming.</u> Bantam Books

Brown, Molly (1997) <u>Growing Whole.</u> Psychosynthesis Press

Hoffman, Bob (1979) <u>No One Is To Blame.</u> Science and Behavior Books, Inc.

Miller, A (1983) <u>For Your Own Good.</u> New York: Farrar Strauss, Giroux.

Perucci. (1983) <u>What We May Be.</u> Putnam Publishing

Pollard, John III (1992) <u>Self-Parenting.</u> Malibu, CA.

Generic Human Studies

Stone, H (1989) <u>Embracing Ourselves.</u> New World Library